New Beginnings...

a novel

DOLORES HIRSCHMANN

Copyright © 2014 Dolores Hirschmann
All rights reserved.
ISBN-13: 978-1497482241
ISBN-10: 1497482240

DEDICATION

To my family,
Alekz, Santiago, Sofia,
Nico, Lukas & Franklin,
who support all my adventures…
even this one.

You are the ones that
make it all possible,
my foundation,
the place where I'm whole.

I love you.

ACKNOWLEDGMENTS

To my mother, *Dotty von Erb*, for being the first eyes to look at this work and the one who encouraged me to bring it out into the world. To *Jane Zimmerman*, who got me writing those long winter nights by the beach, many years ago. To my siblings, my parents, my friends, colleagues, and clients who believed in me and encouraged me along the way. To the Nanowrimo community (www.nanowrimo.com) who posed the challenge that got this book started. To all of you readers who will be spending time with this book, thank you for your time and thank you for sharing it with those in your life.

New Beginnings...

PROLOGUE

As they reached the cliffs at the end of the long stretch of beach, he walked away from the shore to a flat spot where he took a seat, cross-legged, his hands on his knees, palms up.

Lea followed his example and sat next to him, on the warm sand, far away from him so as not to touch but close enough to feel him next to her.

Closing his eyes, he began breathing rhythmically; deep inhales followed by deep exhalations every time. Lea followed his example.

Within seconds they were breathing in synch, the ocean breeze on their face, the salty scent in their nose. There was a physical connection between them that overwhelmed Lea as her body's breathing pattern was taken over by this stranger. Lea allowed herself to relax into it, to be present in it.

Dolores Hirschmann

CHAPTER 1

Lea picked up a magazine as she settled into a faux leather chair in the waiting area. She sat looking out into the street, where the tree-lined road was sprinkled with the first yellow and red fallen leaves of the season. She was early for her appointment, for a change, so she could relax and browse through the latest issue of *People* magazine. As she scanned image after image of beautifully "photoshopped" stars, she glanced at the nails on her right hand and wondered when she would get to them. It had been a month since her last manicure and it was easy to tell. The clear nail polish at the tips of her nails was chipped. Even from a distance one could see where the polish had peeled off leaving rough edges all around the tip of the nail. Since she was a teenager, she had only worn clear nail polish, as she never had the time or patience to deal with her nails on a weekly basis . . .

She sighed as she leafed through the magazine. "Jennifer Lopez is getting a divorce?" she said out loud. As the room was empty, nobody responded. "I thought she just got married, and didn't she just have twins? She looks amazing though," she kept saying, talking to herself.

"Good morning, Mrs. Garris, ready for your appointment?" her hairdresser said as she unfolded a smock for her to wear.

"Yes, of course, good morning, Susan. How are you?" Lea responded while she put down her purse and stretched her arm into the smock.

"I love your outfit, you are always so dressed up," Lea said as she tied the smock on the front while Susan with her long perfectly manicured red nails lifted Lea's hair.

Susan, walking ahead, led Lea into the salon. Her hair, styled with blond hair extensions, fell loosely over her back, her silky skin revealed through her fashionable gray top. Tight skinny jeans shaped her long lean legs with the assistance of six-inch red heels.

"Oh thank you, honey, you are so sweet. You look great too," Susan responded with a smile while she pulled out a chair for her customer.

"Mrs. Garris, would you like anything to drink? Tea, water, coffee . . ." offered Susan as she placed a pile of magazines in front of Lea.

"Susan, please just call me Lea and yes I would love a cup of coffee, no milk or sugar please," said Lea as she placed her left foot on the foot bar while crossing her right leg over and placing the stack of magazines on her lap. Her purse sat on the stylist's counter in front of the mirror.

So her choices were *Vogue, Cosmopolitan, Seventeen, Shape,* or *Yoga Journal.* Lea picked *Yoga Journal* and placed the rest of the magazines on the counter. Susan had brought her a cup of coffee and then proceeded to undo Lea's ponytail while giving instructions to her assistant.

Susan was a very skilled young stylist who had everything going for her. Her versatile hair allowed her to personally showcase anything and everything her salon was capable of doing. If you came every week, you would never see Susan with the same style or even hair color for that matter.

She was tall and lean and wore the most daring outfits in broad daylight and looked perfect for her role. Long red nails complemented her sparkly rings on both hands. She was all for fashion, no doubt, but she was also a very smart businesswoman.

She had left her previous job as a stylist in a small hair salon in Westport, Massachusetts, to open up her own place in Fall River. She had a few followers that transitioned with her, faithful enough to drive the extra twenty minutes to Fall River for her services. At twenty-four, she had an established business with a staff of six people and round the clock hours for her clients.

"So, how's business?" asked Lea while Susan put on her gloves and began applying color to her roots.

"Oh, it's doing great. I just hired a new stylist to help me on Friday and Saturday nights when we have the most customers. It gets so busy . . . I've been looking to add a manicure station and a skin/spa room for facials and massages," she added while expertly applying color on Lea's head, carefully parting her hair to make sure all the gray was covered with the coloring mix.

"I need to get some more color mix—I'll be right back," Susan said as she "*stilettoed*" to the back room for more color solution.

"I think my hair is either growing faster or maybe just the gray hairs are growing faster," Lea commented as Susan came back to finish applying her color. "I think I might need to schedule my appointments four weeks in between instead of six," she added as she watched her stylist finish applying the color and wrap her shoulder-length hair in a plastic cap.

"You might have to. Unfortunately as you get older, the hair does grow faster and the gray hair is thicker, so it shows more through the color. Make sure when we finish today, to make your four-week appointment so we can keep on top of it... After all, you are too young to be walking around with gray hair," Susan said as she led Lea to the dryer for the color to set.

"I know... this getting older is not fun. I'm not even forty. My big birthday is next year, but I can already feel things changing in my body. It's not fun," she muttered more to herself than anything, as the noise of the dryer now muffled her words.

She opened the *Yoga Journal* on her lap and began browsing through the pages. The contents page highlighted an article ***Feel Thirty At Forty***. Lea turned to page twenty-two to read the two-page article.

"Feeling tired? Gray hair growing faster? Need a second cup of coffee to make it through the morning? As we get older, our body is less resilient to put up with our abuses. We can no longer spend the night out drinking and expect to wake up with a smile, nor can we expect that the power of a cup of coffee will keep our aging brain awake for more than an hour. This will

only get worse as the years go by. The only way to stop this is to take control of your body and practice kindness and compassion.

"The time to experiment with our bodies is over. We now have to use our lessons learned, or learn new ones to care for our body the way it expects us to."

She kept reading as she sipped her coffee. Yes, it was true she was more tired these days, especially in the afternoon. Three o'clock for her meant hitting a wall impossible to climb unless she got some sugar and caffeine into her. This had been happening for a while, but for the last three years the need for a quick pick-me-up happened more often. Even though she exercised regularly, she experienced more aches and pains while doing so. She was not completely unhealthy; her recent doctor's checkup had gone well. She had no cholesterol worries nor high blood pressure or anything like that. She did carry a few extra pounds from her last pregnancy, well more than a few, maybe twenty, but while she wished she could lose them, she was not bothered enough to go through the effort.

"... a conscious change in diet and mindset can go a long way toward reversing some of the common symptoms of age, lifting your spirit and giving you back ten years. Whether it is meditation, yoga, healthy eating, or preferably a combination of these, small changes in your daily routine can save you money in medication later on in life and bring new light and energy to

your life, empowering you to be active and enjoy all that life has to offer."

"What is it that you are reading with such concentration?" Susan asked turning off the dryer and lifting the front flap to allow Lea to stand up.

Lea had not heard Susan approaching through the loud hum of the dryer in her ears and was startled.

"Oh, am I done already? That was the fastest twenty minutes ever," Lea said as she folded her magazine, grabbed her and followed Susan to the washing stations.

"This is a good article," Lea pointed to the magazine in her hand. "I have a friend who is in her mid forties and you could never tell. She has the spark and the energy of a much younger person—she always has a smile. I've never seen her moody or upset, and she is running around juggling four children. I sometimes wonder how she does it," Lea continued while Susan rinsed her color and with strong fingers softly massaged the shampoo into Lea's scalp building a lather with the peach-smelling shampoo, her bangles clinking as she worked.

"So how are the kiddos?" Susan asked changing subjects and making conversation. "Is your daughter still giving you a hard time? I can't imagine having a teenage kid in my house, I honestly don't think I am the mother type of person," she continued as she rinsed out the shampoo and applied a good amount of conditioner on Lea's mane.

"Oh, Jenny… she is such a good kid but so stubborn," Lea said as she rolled her eyes thinking of her fifteen-year-old daughter. "Her latest is that she won't wear any jean that is not at least a size smaller than what she needs, so she ends up squeezing into these things that she can barely move in," Lea said with a sigh wondering why girls did that to themselves.

"You should get her the new slim-fit pants from the Gap. They're tight but the stretchy fabric allows you to move. They are pretty cool—I just bought a pair and they are so comfortable. She will love them!" Susan said as she led Lea to the styling chair for final drying and styling.

"That's a good idea. I was planning on going shopping with her this weekend. She has a homecoming dance next weekend and she has *no clothes to wear*, in her clothes-packed closet!" Lea said with a smile.

"Aren't we all the same? I went shopping for shoes the other day to go with my new fall outfits … and I probably own over fifty pairs of shoes!" exclaimed Susan making fun of herself as she blow dried Lea's hair.

"You really have a lot of hair," she said as she worked her fingers through the layers.

Lea's hair had always been thick and plentiful. It had been getting thicker with the years and now, her shoulder-length mane was too much for her to deal with on her own. She hardly ever dried it and had even tried some products to reduce the volume and the frizz.

"I know, I sometimes wish I didn't have so much," Lea said watching Susan's muscle in her upper right arm tighten as she worked the brush and pulled her hair down while her left hand worked the dryer over her stretched hair.

"So how are your other ventures going?" Lea asked as she checked herself in the mirror, most of her hair now dried and styled.

"Oh, everything is going well, my husband decided to start a new business—just what we needed—but he is doing very well so he's happy," Susan said as she grabbed the last chunk of hair and worked her way through it.

Susan not only owned and ran her hair salon but she was a full-on entrepreneur from an early age. She and her husband owned a few franchise businesses in Fall River ranging from fast food to rental cars.

"I'm impressed that with all the work you have going

on you always look amazing," Lea commented again somehow jealous of her stylist's youth and looks.

"Thank you, Lea, it's my business to look good. I enjoy it but I also know that looking good is part of my job," Susan explained as she rubbed some styling mousse between her hands and applied it to Lea's head for a finishing touch.

"There you go, all done. Maybe next time we'll trim the ends, your hair is getting long," Susan said as she untied the protective bib and put the dryer back into the drawer as Lea slipped off the smock.

"Thank you, as always it looks great. Hope I can keep it up at home," Lea said with a smile. "I'll make a four-week appointment to stay on top of the gray," she continued as she grabbed her purse and walked to the coat closet to get her vest.

"Thanks, Lea," waved Susan as she courteously ushered another client over to the styling station.

It was late October and while the weather had been warm until a few days earlier, it had suddenly changed, forcing Lea to add an extra layer of clothing. She had yet to clean her closet and make the summer – winter switch so in the meantime she just layered long-sleeve T-shirts under her down vest that she always kept in the downstairs closet by the front door.

"Thank you, Mrs. Garris," said the receptionist as she

handed Lea her receipt, credit card, and her appointment card for her next visit.

"Thank you and Happy Halloween," Lea said as she took her sunglasses from her purse and walked out the door.

CHAPTER 2

Lea was running late to meet the kids coming home from school. They had recently switched to the neighborhood public school, and Lea loved that they would come and go from school in a bus.

For a few years the three of them were attending a private school half an hour away from home and without any carpool connections, Lea and her husband had been driving the kids to and from school every day.

She missed the driving time; she realized now that she had enjoyed it. She would use the time to check in with friends, talk with her mother who now lived in New York, or listen to some audio books, usually the book of the month that she never had time to read for her book club.

She drove at the highest speed limit trying to make up for lost time. While the salon was only ten minutes from her house, she was already five minutes beyond the kids' usual arrival time. She was hoping that Jenny, her oldest daughter, was already home as high school let out early some days, but she could not remember if this was one of those days. While Jenny who was in high school and Colin who was in middle school could get off the bus at their house even if she was not there, little Lauren, who was still in elementary school, needed to have one of her parents or her sister be at the stop in order for the bus driver to let her get off the bus.

As she approached the house, she saw Lauren's bus coming from the other direction; she honked and waved to the bus driver as she made her way into their driveway. Her oldest daughter was nowhere to be seen.

Lauren got out of the bus and ran to her mother as Lea got out of her car and bent down to hug her, one hand waving to the bus driver.

Once Lauren was settled in the kitchen with a snack, Lea tried calling her long-time friend from high school who now lived in Argentina but the line was busy. She had sent her a quick email while driving home from the salon, her left hand on the steering wheel, her right hand typing the email while her eyes constantly tried to keep an eye on the road. It was a dangerous habit and she knew it. When the kids were in the car, she usually kept her phone in the glove compartment, away from her, so as not to be tempted.

"Mum, did you get the stuff I need for science?" were her teenage daughter's first words as she walked in the house banging the mudroom door as she dropped her backpack and took off her shoes.

"In the kitchen . . . Jenny how was your day?" Lea said with a forced smile trying not to react to her daughter's demanding tone and hoping for a smooth afternoon. "I did get your stuff. It's here in the kitchen," she said as she grabbed a shopping bag full of tapes and supplies she had picked up for her daughter and placed it in the middle of the counter.

"Hey, don't push," said Jenny blocking the hallway with her backpack as Colin ran in the house. She had grown a lot the last year and now she was taller than Lea and was wearing shoes size 9. She was a fully developed young woman and was still trying to find herself in this new body.

"Hello Mum, I'm starving," said Colin ignoring his

sister's warning and pushing her out of his way as he ran in on his way to the kitchen, dumping his sweatshirt, lunchbox, backpack, gym bag, and instrument on the floor in the middle of the kitchen.

"Ommm," Lea chanted to herself as she watched her older children overtake the kitchen. "Here we go," she said in a whisper as she took a deep breath and gathered her energy to intervene before Jenny reacted to Colin's storming past her.

"Hi, Colin. Hey, can you please put your things in the mudroom?" Lea asked looking at the pile of stuff now lying by her feet.

Missy, their golden retriever, joined them in the kitchen, her tail wagging with excitement at the sight of her family.

"Mummy, guess what? I got an A in my science test," Lauren said with a smile as she finished her snack, oblivious to the chaos around her.

"That's great, Lauren, congratulations. You are such a smart girl," Lea said smiling at her little girl and trying to stay in control of the older kids. Lauren was still in that little girl phase where she was for the most part happy and always excited to see her mother at the end of the day. Lea knew it wouldn't last; she had experienced it with Jenny, but for now she cherished every second of it.

"Mum, remember I have soccer at five this afternoon, right?" said Colin as he opened the pantry and proceeded to grab cookies and snacks while complaining that his mother had not packed extra snacks for him in his lunchbox.

"Yes, I know, I spoke with John's mum and they will pick you up at four-forty-five and then his dad will bring both of you back at six-thirty," said Lea proud of herself for having made a plan so that she did not need to go out and drive Colin to his practice.

Afternoons were getting more and more challenging with every new school year. Jenny had after-school activities that were hard to manage with the other kids' schedule. Colin had soccer practice twice a week, and now Lauren had ballet twice a week. So between their schedules, making dinner, and helping everyone get their schoolwork done, Lea felt like she spent her day getting ready for her evening.

"Mummy, remember I have a project due tomorrow. I have to make a poster board about the pilgrims," Lauren said as she placed her snack's wrapper in the trash and grabbing her backpack headed toward the study area right off the kitchen.

"I'm still hungry," Colin said as he brought his books and papers to the kitchen table with a thump.

"Colin, please take off your shoes and leave them in

the mudroom. You can have a piece of fruit if you are still hungry—you already had two snacks," Lea said as she began emptying the kid's lunchboxes that the children had deposited all over the counter.

"Jenny, you did not touch your sandwich. Was there other food for lunch today?" Lea asked her teenage daughter, concerned that she had been very picky about food lately.

"No, I don't like peanut butter and jelly, and I didn't have time anyway. Can you just pack some sugar free Jell-O and fruit? That's all I want," she said dismissing her mother's concern and taking her schoolwork up to her room.

"No I can NOT pack you a Jell-O and fruit, that's not enough food to keep you going," Lea said in a whisper knowing her daughter had already left the room.

"Mummy, do we have a poster board so I can start my project?" Lauren said as she brought her schoolwork to the counter where Lea was now cleaning up the dishes from breakfast and loading up the dishwasher. She had been out most of the day and had not been able to clean up after breakfast.

"Oh, Lauren, I forgot about the poster board. I thought that project was due next week," Lea said apologetically.

"No, it's due tomorrow," Lauren, said, her eyes starting to well up with tears.

"OK, let's do this. Let's look up all the information, make pictures, print maps, and then we will ask Daddy to get one on the way home tonight and I'll help you put it all together. How does that sound?" Lea said as she dried her hands on a dishtowel and picked up her daughter. She took a seat and held Lauren on her lap. Lauren wrapped her little arms around her neck and pressed her warm face against Lea's.

"OK, we'll do that," Lauren said, welcoming her mother's embrace.

"Mum, where's my soccer shirt. Is it in the dryer?" Colin yelled from upstairs.

"Oh my gosh, it's four-thirty already! No, it's in the laundry room," Lea said jumping up and rushing to the laundry room, making Lauren slip off her lap. She thought she had started a load that morning but she was not sure.

"Colin, I got your shirt and shorts in the washing machine this morning, but I forgot to start it. They have been sitting there all day with the other dirty laundry… They are all wet and stinky!" Lea said pouring soap into the detergent compartment and starting the load.

"Mum, I don't have any other clothes, remember? I lost my other set last weekend!" Colin now screamed from upstairs, upset that he was running late and wondering what he would wear.

"Grab a pair of shorts from your sister. She has some black ones and just wear any shirt. It's not a big deal, it's just practice," Lea said as she hurried up the stairs.

"I can't, the coach is going to yell at me. I need my soccer uniform." Colin said as his mother walked into his room trying to avoid the clothes, toys, and books scattered all over the floor.

"Well, you have no choice. I'm sure it happens to other kids as well. Just get dressed, John's mum will be here any minute now," Lea said not willing to engage in a blaming game. She already felt frazzled and the kids had only been home for two hours. Her self-soothing "ommm" was no longer working for her.

Colin, having found a shirt and shorts, pushed past her on his way down the stairs as his friend knocked on the mudroom door.

"Bye, Mum," he said as he closed the door with a thump.

"Oh well, one fire out, what's next?" Lea muttered to herself as she picked up the clothes her son left all over his bedroom floor in a rush to get out the door.

"Mum, what am I going to wear Friday night for the homecoming dance? I have nothing to wear!" Jenny yelled from her room.

Their house was large enough to provide each child with a room, a luxury Lea did not have growing up.

"I thought you were doing your homework," Lea said as she walked into her daughter's room to find clothes piled on the bed, on the floor, everywhere.

"I was, but Molly texted me asking what I was going to wear Friday night and to see if I could sleep over at her house that night. Can I, Mum? Her dad will pick us up from the dance and then I can be home by noon on Saturday in time for my soccer game," Jenny said as she kept pulling clothes from hangers.

"OK, hold on, stop pulling things from your closet. You know you'll have to clean this whole mess up anyway," Lea said barely containing her anger. She had always struggled with her daughter's moody personality. It was all or nothing for her... they had warned her when she was pregnant.

The old mothers would say, "Uhhh, I hope you have a boy. Boys are active at the beginning but so much simpler in the end. Daughters can drive you crazy!"

She now understood their comments. While she loved Jenny like any mother loves her child, sometimes Jenny brought out the worst in her.

"OK, what is Molly wearing for the party?" Lea asked starting from the beginning. If she could get Jenny talking about the event and what her friends were planning to wear, she would be able to lower her anxiety and start working toward a solution. Clothes' shopping was out of the question that night, and tomorrow it would be too late by the time she came home from school.

"They are all wearing dresses—I don't have any dresses," Jenny said with a pout and throwing herself on her bright green bean bag even though it was covered with clothes. Her arms were crossed over her chest, her body language for "I'm upset and there is nothing you can do about it."

"OK, let's start putting together some options and see if any of them might work. You have the new skirt we got last week, with the gray and black ruffles; you could pair that with the white cowl-neck top. Tights and boot would go great with that," Lea said.

"No, the skirt is too short and my legs are fat," Jenny responded refusing to move from her seat or uncross her arms or ... open her mind to a solution.

"Hi, guys," said Paul walking up the stairs.

"Oh, Paul, is it six o'clock already or are you home early?" Lea said surprised by her husband's arrival.

"Yes, it's six o'clock. What's going on here? Are we

moving? I'm starving, should Lauren and I set the table?" Paul continued taking in his teenage daughter's room and the fact that there was no sign of any meal being prepped in the kitchen.

"Oh no, dinner… I lost track of time and I also forgot to call you to pick up a poster board for Lauren's project on your way home from work. It's been a tough afternoon," Lea then walked out of Jenny's room taking large strides to avoid the piles of clothes everywhere.

"Jenny, please pick up your clothes, finish your homework, and we'll figure out your outfit after dinner," Lea said as she walked out, refusing to deal with Jenny any longer.

"Lea, let me help," said Paul, recognizing his wife's overwhelmed state and the fact that if he did not step in there would be no dinner, no project finished, or anything.

"Thanks," Lea said recognizing her defeat.

"I'll head out and get a pizza when I pick up Lauren's poster board," Paul said walking out the door before finishing his sentence.

Lea took a seat next to her daughter, "Lauren, honey, how are you coming with your research?"

"Look, Mummy, I found all this stuff on the Internet.

Can we print it? And I did these two pictures," Lauren said with her sweet eight-year-old voice.

Lea never thought she would miss the sleepless nights and the hard work required when her children were young, but after the afternoon she just had, she wished her teenagers were still sweet and cuddly, children who would want to sit on her lap at the end of the day. Such a contrast between Lauren's sweet little-girl disposition and the attitude of her older children.

"That's great, Lauren, Daddy just went to get your poster board. Why don't you go get a shower and get into pajamas so that we can finish your project when Daddy comes back? Does that sound like a good plan?" Lauren put down her pencils and walked up the stairs to the bathroom.

"Hi Mum," came Colin's voice as he slammed the door on his way in from soccer. "What's for dinner, I'm starving," he said as he took off his cleats and left them right in the middle of the mudroom.

"Hi Colin, how was practice? Wow, were the fields that wet— you are covered in mud," Lea said as her son trailed mud through the corridor on his way to the kitchen.

"Stop right there. Please go back into the laundry room and take off your socks, your shirt, and your shorts and then go up and have a shower before you get mud all over the house," she said intercepting him and guiding him to the laundry room that was right next to the mudroom. The day had been long enough already; she did not need mud everywhere on top of it.

Colin complained, "But Mum…" He followed his mother's instructions knowing he had no choice.

Lea went back to the kitchen, pulled a pile of plates and cups from the dishwasher and set the table for dinner. Pizza was not the healthiest choice for her family, but she had no energy for anything else tonight.

From the fridge she pulled a bag of prewashed greens and some carrots and put together a quick salad. She brought forks, the salad, and dressing to the table.

"Ready, Mum," Lauren said coming into the kitchen in her pink slipper pajamas looking all warm and cozy. She had washed her hair and pulled it in a tight ponytail.

"Hmm, you smell so good," Lea, pressed her nose on her daughter's head as she gave her a big hug.

"Dinner's ready," said her husband's deep voice as he closed the mudroom door and walked into the kitchen. In his right hand he carried two boxes of pizza, and a poster board was pressed under his left arm.

"That smells good," said Colin now walking into the kitchen all clean and buttoning up his pajamas.

"I hate store-bought pizza," were Jenny's words as she walked into the kitchen and sat at the table.

"Now, Jenny, please don't use that word, how many times do we need to remind you that there is no need to use that word; it's not kind," Paul said in his patient voice.

"So, Lauren, what is your project about?" Paul asked as the whole family came to the kitchen table. They all settled down, grabbed some salad and a slice of pizza while Lea poured water from the pitcher.

"Jenny, if you are only going to eat salad, please put some cheese or some cold cuts on it. You can't just have greens, you need some protein," Lea said noticing her daughter had not helped herself to pizza.

"OK, Mum," Jenny said as she uncurled her feet from under herself and walked to the fridge.

"It's about the pilgrims," Lauren said looking at her father with her big green eyes. "I already did all the pictures and printed the information I need. I just have to glue it all on the poster," she continued as she chewed her pizza slice.

Lauren had her mother's eyes. Everyone said so. Her

dark curly hair, porcelain skin, and green eyes were a true mirror of her mother's.

"Perfect, then I'll help you after dinner, OK?" Paul said as he put some salad on his plate.

"So Mum, can I sleep over at Molly's tomorrow after the party?" Jenny asked as she sat with her right leg under her butt and chewed with her mouth open holding her fork like a pencil.

"Jenny, please sit properly," her father said as Lea rolled her eyes. It was amazing how the older she got the more she refused to follow basic house manners and rules.

"I don't see why not, Jenny. Your soccer game on Saturday is not until two in the afternoon, right?" Lea asked, actually looking forward to not having to pick up her daughter at eleven at night after the dance. They had known her friend Molly since they were little girls and they trusted her parents to be on time and keep an eye on them.

"Colin, do you have a soccer game this weekend?" Paul asked as Jenny picked up her plate and brought it to the sink.

"Yes, we're playing Fall River. We played them earlier in the season and we lost so we are hoping for a win this weekend. The game is at ten on Saturday morning in Fall River, can you come watch it?" Colin asked looking at his father and hoping he would be able to watch him play.

Paul tried hard to be an active part of his children's life, He was a good father, but sometimes his travel schedule kept him out of town on weekends. As head of the legal department of a multinational company, he traveled frequently across the country and sometimes internationally.

"Yes, of course, I would love it. You can tell John that if his parents can't take him we will pick him up and take him. Maybe we can go out for lunch after the game. There's a good place for burgers in Fall River I've been wanting to try out," Paul said making a plan with his son.

"Well, Lauren, I guess it's you and me Saturday morning. What should we do?" Lea said looking at her youngest daughter as she finished her pizza.

"Well, actually, Isabel asked if I could have a play date and sleepover after school tomorrow," Lauren said with begging eyes.

"Sure, honey," Lea said feeling a little sad that she would not have anyone to hang out with on Saturday morning. Isabel was a good friend of Lauren's. They did ballet together and often planned sleepovers on weekends.

Lea picked up her plate, the salad bowl, and the pizza

boxes and took them to the kitchen sink. Her husband opened the dishwasher door to start loading but realized it was full with clean dishes.

"I'll do it," Lea said, "You go help Lauren with her homework," she continued as she began pulling dishes from the dishwasher.

"Are you OK?" Paul asked as he kissed her neck sweetly. "You look stressed," he said as he smiled and insisted on Lea turning around to hug him.

"I'm just tired," Lea said not responding to his seducing tactics.

"Daddy, look what I found! I have the glue and all this information to put on the board, "Lauren said coming toward her father eager to get her project going.

"Let me see," Paul said as he released Lea and went with Lauren to the desk where she had laid out all her material.

No way, Lea thought to herself recognizing the kiss as a sign that her husband would be looking for something else later that night. *All I want is to crawl into bed and read my book tonight*, She finished emptying the dishwasher and cleaning up after dinner.

CHAPTER 3

It was Saturday night and Lea pulled out pizza crust, cheese, pizza sauce, and tomatoes.

"Who wants to come make their own pizzas?" she said from the kitchen counter to her children scattered all over the house. Jenny was in her room, face timing her friends, Lauren was watching TV downstairs in the family playroom, and Colin was playing a video game while listening to his iPod touch.

Nobody answered.

"OK, then I'll make them however I want," she threatened as she opened a can of pizza sauce and began spreading the pizza crusts with sauce. She had given up on family-size crusts, as each one of her children would complain about compromising to the other one's taste.

Jenny did not like spices, Colin would not take tomato on his pizza and Lauren wanted a minimum amount of cheese.

"I'm coming, Mum," Lauren said expertly using the TV control to pause her show. "Can I have pineapple and ham on mine. I tried that at Isabel's house and it tastes great," she said surprising Lea with her strange request.

"Hmm, that sounds interesting, I think at the pizza shop they call it Hawaiian. I don't have pineapple, but maybe next week we can try that," Lea said giving up on her older children and preparing their pizzas while Lauren began carefully arranging tomato slices.

"Lauren, Dad and I are going out tonight. Karla is coming to babysit. You can watch TV until eight-thirty, but then you need to go to bed. We are going up to your grandparents for lunch tomorrow so we need to be ready and out the door by 10 AM," she said while she loaded the oven and cleaned up the counter.

"I love Karla," Lauren said as she pressed play on her show and sat again on the couch by the TV.

Karla had been a mother's helper at first; coming one

or two afternoons a week to stay with Lauren while Lea drove Jenny and Colin around. With seven years difference between her older daughter and her baby girl, as she liked to think about Lauren, she had needed someone to stay in the house with the baby while she drove Jenny to ballet, gymnastics, and everything in between.

Karla had now graduated from college and was a stunning twenty-two-year-old young woman. While she had moved to New York to work at a fashion magazine, her dream since she was a little girl, she had been forced to move back home with her parents as her mother was dealing with breast cancer, her second time around, and this time it did not look like she was going to make it.

"Pizza is ready!" Lea said as she heard the mudroom door open and close.

"Good afternoon, Mrs. Garris," Karla said as she took off her down vest and hung it on the back of a chair by the counter.

"Oh, hi Karla. Right on time. Would you like some pizza? I can throw in another one if you want," Lea said as her other children came into the kitchen for their dinner.

"No, thank you. I'm all set. I just had dinner with my mother before I came," she said hugging Lauren who had intercepted her halfway into the kitchen.

"How is your mum? I was planning to come by and visit with her some time this week. How is she doing with the experimental treatment?" Lea asked now focusing her attention on Karla.

"Well, some days are better than others. She is very weak though and that keeps her mostly indoors. I've rented a wheelchair so I can take her out for some fresh air when the days are not too cold. I want to make sure she gets out as much as she can before winter comes. It's going to be harder as it gets colder." A hint of the ordeal she was going through could be detected in her tone.

"Please let me know if you need anything. I know your dad is traveling and I'm sure it's a lot for you to bear alone," Lea said wishing there was more she could do.

"Thank you, Mrs. Garris. These are the days I wish I had siblings. At least my mum's sister helps a lot, and she is spending the weekend with us so that I can get out," Karla said as Lauren, having finished her pizza, was pulling on her arm to go play a board game with her.

"Paul, let's go. The movie starts at six-thirty," Lea yelled from the bottom of the stairs as she slipped on her green and pink polka dot rain boots. It was raining and while she felt like crawling in bed with a good book, she had decided that she and Paul needed to go out at least once a month. She felt that in the last year or so their relationship had been put aside in favor of the daily juggling of everybody else's schedule.

"I'm coming," Paul said as he came down the stairs buttoning his shirt. That afternoon he had been working outside cleaning up and getting the yard ready for the winter months. His hair, a dark thick mane, was still wet from the shower. Though he had just had his forty-fifth birthday, he had hardly any gray hair. A few were popping up on the sides, right above his sideburns, but other than that, his tall slim build and deep-set blue eyes together with his full head of hair made him look much younger.

"So, what is it that we are watching tonight?" he asked as he grabbed his rain jacket from the hook in the mudroom and closed the door behind them.

"We talked about it this morning—the latest movie with Matt Damon," Lea said sounding a little irritated. She knew that her husband would also rather get in pajamas and hang out at home with the kids and watch TV than go out. She knew it was not about spending time with her but he just liked being at home, specially on a rainy day.

Paul's car was in the garage, right next to the

mudroom door, so they did not need to get wet getting in. Lea hopped in the passenger seat as Paul pressed the garage door opener and reversed the car into the driveway.

"We don't have much time to get something to eat before the movie," Lea said as they drove down the street, past their neighbor's house and into the main road that led to the mall, where the movie theater was.

"I'm OK, I had some food before I showered," Paul said without further conversation.

As they pulled into the mall, they could see a long line to get tickets, so Paul dropped Lea off while he parked the car.

It seemed like everyone had the same idea tonight. Lea ran into a few people she knew from soccer, ballet, and the PTO *(Parent Teacher Organization)* while she waited for her husband in the ticket line.

By the time the movie was over it was nine-thirty and pitch dark outside. The rain had slowed down and as the temperature had dropped the light drizzle became a mix of rain and sleet.

"Let's go to the coffee shop next door," Lea suggested as they headed for the exit of the theater. "I'm hungry now." She zipped up her jacket against the cold wind outside. There was a covered walkway to the coffee shop.

"So, did you like the movie? Matt Damon does not make a movie a year like many of the other actors but when he does work in a movie it's usually very good. I think he is one of the most serious actors out there," Lea said as her husband opened the door for her and they walked to the back of the shop to find a place by the fireplace.

The coffee shop had been open for a few years and it was nice when you could find an empty sofa next to the gas fireplace. It was inviting and relaxing and Paul and Lea enjoyed the casual dining aspect.

While they were dating they would often go out for dinner, after all they lived in New York for most of their dating time. They enjoyed trying new restaurants and meeting friends for dinner. They had stayed in New York until Jenny was born. Lea used to work for a fashion magazine. She was the assistant to the fashion editor and enjoyed being part of the New York fashion world. Paul as a lawyer worked in a private practice mostly in corporate law. They enjoyed a good life but were not wealthy by any means. When Jenny was born, Lea stayed home with her for the first six months and then she tried going back to work. She had worked long enough at the magazine that they allowed her to work from home a few days a week, but they did not have much luck with nannies and babysitters. By the time Jenny was one and a half

Lea decided that she had had enough juggling work and incompetent help. She quit her job and stayed home full time. Living on one paycheck in New York was harder than they thought, and by the time Lea was pregnant with Colin they decided to move to Massachusetts. Here they could afford a house with a backyard and the kids could go to the local public school. They settled into the typical suburban family life.

Lea had not gone back to work. She was kept busy with PTO, fundraising events, and driving the kids back and forth. Paul had done well in the corporate world joining a multinational company that happened to have its headquarters in Fall River.

Paul and Lea were happy to find that the area around the fireplace was available and placed their coats on a sofa to reserve their space before heading to the counter to order their food.

Panera was a perfect place for them. The food was good, it was not expensive, and, it was close to home. They enjoyed trying out the different salads and seasonal sandwiches.

"I'll have the chicken salad, please," said Lea to the cashier.

"And I'll have bean soup and half a sandwich," Paul said as he pulled out his wallet and gave the girl his credit card.

"Anything to drink? For here or to go?" the cashier asked as her long purple Halloween nails pushed buttons on the cash register.

They ordered sparkling water and a Coke.

"Thank you. They'll call your number on the receipt when your order is ready," the attendant said as she handed Paul back his credit card and receipt.

They headed back to the fireplace and settled back into the sofa.

Paul told Lea about the soccer match. "I watched Colin play today. The game was over before the rain started it was cold but he did great. He was so excited for his team to win. Next week they are playing against Rochester Team."

"That's great. It was nice having the kids out for the night last night. Too bad you had to work late," Lea said with a hint of reproach.

"I know, there was not much I could do. We needed to finish the contract with this new company they are acquiring, and it's going to be busy for a while. I might have to go to Italy in the next few weeks to finalize papers," Paul said.

Italy? I would love to come too, thought Lea to herself. She knew it was impossible for the two of them to leave the kids, but she wished it were easier.

"Number thirty-two," shouted the guy behind the counter as he placed two oval-shaped dishes on the counter.

"I'll get it," Paul said getting up before Lea had a chance to uncurl herself from the sofa.

"Hmm, I'm so hungry," she said as her husband placed her salad on the table in front of her.

"So, Jenny is not doing great at school right now. Her grades are slipping in both math and science. She is at such a difficult stage that I don't want to interfere too much as it might be counterproductive, but I feel she needs some help. She and I don't always see eye to eye," Lea said as she filled her fork with greens and a piece of chicken.

"OK, I'll see if I can sit with her tomorrow and help her with homework. She can sometimes get stuck in the silliest things and if need be, we might need to cut back on outings, computer time, et cetera, so that she can focus on her work," Paul said as he blew on his spoon before trying his soup.

Even though they tried to spend time together, their conversations focused on the kids, their schedule or school issues, the house, and the bills. To observers, they seemed like a well-adjusted couple, but they both felt lonely at times.

Lea missed their light conversations about politics, dreams, and the world in general. Paul was too focused on providing for his family that he didn't even realize he was content but not happy. They plowed along, like two people sitting next to each other on a train ride. They were respectful and polite to each other; some might say they loved each other, in that comfortable way of couples that settles into a routine of love. But there was little passion these days and Lea missed it. Lea needed to feel that spark again when she looked into her husband's eyes.

He was handsome, no doubt about it, but his eyes looked tired, he did not smile much, and he looked disheartened.

"Maybe I should coach Colin's basketball team this winter," Paul said with some excitement in his voice."

"That would be wonderful!" she said encouraging this new idea. "I think Colin would love it and it would be good for you to hang out with the kids and connect with other guys, but can you make the time commitment?"

"I think I can pull it off, specially if I can coach with some other dad and we can back each other up if one of us can't make it," Paul said suddenly excited about something for a change.

"That would be great," Lea said genuinely smiling for

the first time that night.

"Yes," Paul said as he shifted his focus back to his sandwich.

Lea was surprised but pleased by Paul's initiative. Maybe getting to connect with some of the other fathers would get them to socialize more, maybe go out with other couples. She was not sure what she was looking for, but she knew she needed something. She needed to find herself, and she needed a better relationship with her husband in the midst of their daily life. She sometimes worried that if they didn't try to find their spark that their world, Lea and Paul's micro world, would at some point shrink to nothing. The only things that they shared would be their kids' schedules and school work their house and their bills.

CHAPTER 4

Lea ran after her son as he ran out to get the school bus. "Don't forget your lunchbox," she called as she followed in her bathrobe and slippers.

"Thanks, Mum," Colin said turning red, as his mum had made it all the way to the street just as the bus pulled up, full of kids. Their stop was one of the last ones. Jenny had already left in her high school bus.

"Bye, Colin," Lea said as she picked up the newspaper from the frosty ground and made her way back to the house. It was seven-thirty on a cold October morning and her two older kids were already on their way to school.

Lauren sat at the kitchen counter finishing up her cereal. Lea turned her attention to the last lunchbox of the morning. "Do you want apples or grapes?" she asked her daughter as she grabbed a container from the drawer and bent down in a frustrating search for its lid.

"Grapes," Lauren said as she picked up her bowl and drank the milk right from the edge as she came down the stool and headed upstairs to brush her teeth and comb her hair.

"Don't forget to grab a sweater," Lea said as Lauren disappeared up the stairs. Lea sipped her second cup of coffee, her hip resting against the granite kitchen counter, both hands on the mug as she listened for Lauren upstairs.

"Bye, Mum," Lauren called as she rushed out the door, bringing her mother back to earth.

"Have a good day," Lea said as she walked to the side door and watched her daughter run down the driveway to the corner to wait for the bus, her backpack and lunchbox bouncing behind her as she ran, almost covering most of her body. Lea watched from the side door, with her shoulder leaning against the doorframe, her arms crossed at her chest.

Once the bus picked up Lauren, Lea went back into

the house and closed the door behind her. She sat at the kitchen table with her cup of coffee and the paper. She sat there scanning the front page, enjoying the sudden silence in the house, embracing the warmth of her drink.

As she finished her coffee she looked up at the clock on the stove and realized she only had fifteen minutes to get out the door. Putting the cup in the sink and shoving the bowls and plates from breakfast on top of the already half-filled sink she ran upstairs to change. She found her exercise clothes, still on the floor where she had left them last Friday, and put them on, spraying some flowery mist on top to disguise any hint of smell on her sweaty top.

She grabbed her hair in a low ponytail and quickly brushed her teeth.

Lea had signed up with a trainer a few weeks ago and she had scheduled appointments with her three times a week.

"Sorry I'm late," she said as she ran into the gym.

"Not too bad," Rebecca said as she grabbed a paper clip and Lea's chart and led her client to the back room where the elliptical and running machines were.

"Let's start with a ten-minute warm-up on the elliptical," she said as she pressed a few buttons to set up the machine while Lea hopped on.

"So how was your weekend?" Rebecca asked as the machine began to move forcing Lea to walk and move her arms at the same time.

"Not bad. I can't believe how much rain we got on Saturday," she said finding her pace.

"Were you able to watch what you ate?" Rebecca asked lifting an eyebrow as she looked at Lea.

"Well, more or less. It's so hard with the kids' crazy schedules and going out and candy everywhere even if Halloween is not for another two weeks," Lea said now sounding breathless as her heart rate went up with every stride.

"Well, no fight no gain," Rebecca said making notes on her paper. "You know that if you want to lose those twenty pounds you need to watch everything you eat. You can't just say 'Oh a candy here, a candy there.' That won't cut it. You know that the older you get the harder it's going to be, so the sooner you do it the better," Rebecca continued as she pressed some more buttons when the machine beeped at the ten-minute mark.

"I know, I know," said Lea, as she had heard it all before.

"Let's see what the scale has to say," Rebecca said leading Lea to the nearest scale. There were a few of them placed along the back wall of the gym where the trainers weighed their "victims."

"That's not fair… I just had some water, and I had two coffees this morning," Lea said dreading it.

At five feet eight she had never been very light. She always felt like a giant next to most of her friends and her husband, taller than she, was very skinny.

"One seventy-five. You can do better than that Lea," Rebecca said taking notes on her chart. "At least you are down a pound from last Monday but at this rate we will never reach our goal of twenty pounds by Christmas," she reminded her.

"I know. I can't believe I'm that heavy! For most of my teenage years and early twenties I stayed around one fifty pounds or so; I was a size six. Now I'm a size twelve and I hate it," Lea said stepping down from the scale and following her trainer to the weight room.

"OK, let's not focus on that. You are healthy and beautiful, and we will tone that body while you lose your weight. You should start feeling better independent of your weight. As you build muscle, you will be able to control hunger better, and your metabolism will work faster, so let's not cry over spilled milk— let's do something about it," Rebecca said changing the tone of the conversation and giving Lea two ten-pound dumbbells as she demonstrated the squat exercise she wanted her to do.

"Don't cry over spilled milk?" Lea smiled as she began her squatting series. "My grandmother used to say that. She was born in England and came here to the US in her twenties after the Second World War. Her sister, a nurse in the war, had married a US soldier, and they had moved to New York. She came and stayed with them for a year or so and then met and married my grandfather, a lawyer in New York," Lea said as her trainer counted out loud.

"Well, my grandmother is Irish, so maybe that's where I got it from," Rebecca said smiling.

"Do you have any big plans for Thanksgiving?" Lea said making conversation as she finished her last squat, her legs shaking as she tried to keep her mind off her pain.

"I'll tell you while you do fifteen jumping jacks, touching the ground," Rebecca said as she demonstrated the move to Lea.

"Not fair," she complained as she started the jumping jacks.

"Faster," Rebecca said.

"My boyfriend and I are going to spend Thanksgiving with his parents in New Hampshire. This is the first time I'm formally invited to a family gathering. His three sisters and their husbands will be there as well as some of his nieces and nephews. I'm a little nervous about the whole thing. We've been dating for two years and I think he is the one. I'm actually hoping for a proposal any time now… Two more," Rebecca said as she began setting up a step with two risers on each side for Lea to do some stepping exercises.

"How can you talk and count at the same time!" Lea exclaimed.

"A gift I have," Rebecca said as she demonstrated the next exercise using two five-pound dumbbells.

Rebecca was in her late twenties; small framed and toned with a commanding air about her—perfect for her role as a personal trainer.

"That's nice. You'll do great," Lea said referring to Rebecca's upcoming plans. "Who knows, maybe you'll be engaged by the end of the year," Lea added. "I remember when Paul and I were dating. I was finishing my last year at NYU when we met. He was working at a law office in New York. He was a friend of my roommate's brother and when he came into the city for work interviews, he invited his sister and me out for dinner and Paul came along. I remember those first dates, the butterflies in my stomach, the excitement of whether or not he would call me the next day…" Lea said almost talking to herself.

"Does he have a big family?" Rebecca asked as Lea laid on her back on a mat on the floor, and Rebecca stretched her legs using her own body weight for a deeper stretch of her client's limbs.

"Uhh, that feels good," Lea murmured closing her eyes. "Yes, but his parents live in Florida, and his three siblings are spread all around. He is the oldest while I'm the baby in my family. At the time I think his youngest brother was still in high school in Florida while his other brother and sister were in school somewhere on the West Coast. I didn't get to meet any of them until after we had been dating for over a year," Lea said, now getting off the mat, drinking a sip of water from her water bottle, and helping Rebecca clean up the equipment as they finished the session.

"Good work today. Keep drinking water through the day to help the muscles recover and keep an eye on what you eat. Don't buy any Halloween candy until that day and if you can buy stuff you don't like—that's even better—so that you don't get tempted," Rebecca reminded Lea as she walked her to the door.

Lea zipped up her coat as she exited the building and using the automatic door opener she clicked her car open and hopped in.

As she drove around doing errands, picking up her husband's dry cleaning and getting some groceries, she remembered those first few years in New York with Paul.

She was twenty-one when they met and by the time she turned twenty-two they were sharing a small apartment in the Village. She was lucky to find a job as a fashion editor assistant at Vogue Magazine almost as soon as she finished school. She had interned with another magazine the previous summer and her boss had transferred to Vogue, so by mere chance, her first job had been her teenage girl dream job.

While the paycheck was modest to say the least, the job came with great perks. She had amazing discounts to many fashion designers and her size six allowed her to keep a lot of the clothes left over from photo shoots, especially items that the designers had not bothered to pick up. Most of the girls around her were either bigger or much smaller and, while some of the models they used for the shoots were size two or size four, they sometimes had no choice in the size the designers sent for the shoots, and they had to make do with size six clothing.

She remembered those years as some of the best; she was independent but still sharing life with her wonderfully handsome boyfriend. Her coworkers would all go crazy when he picked her up from work, as they thought he was really handsome. One of the photographers even asked if he would be willing to pose for a shoot once as they needed an extra to pose with the models, and he looked just like what they were looking for.

She remembered when she asked him about it.

"No way," had been his first words as they were finishing breakfast before work.

"But it's going to be so much fun. I'll be there helping out and I promise you won't have to wear anything weird. Just jeans and a white shirt." She had pleaded with him hoping he'd give in.

"No way. Have you ever seen a good, successful lawyer that also appears in fashion magazines? My colleagues would have a huge laugh, and I don't think the partners will view me as a serious future partner," he had said closing the newspaper and getting ready to go. At the time he was hoping to become a partner at his firm.

Lea smiled remembering those days as she parked at the cleaners to get his shirts. She had so much wanted him to pose, but she understood his point. Models and lawyers don't always go hand in hand.

She pulled into the garage as she got back home, and getting the shirts and the few groceries from the car, she went into the house to shower and change.

As soon as she walked in her smile faded. She was reminded of her current life, the beds to be made, the kitchen to clean, baskets full of laundry to fold, and Missy, greeting her at the door and needing a walk.

She dropped the bags of groceries in the kitchen and headed up the stairs to her bedroom. She hung the shirts, each covered with a plastic bag, on her husband's side of the closet, and then she walked into the bathroom.

In the shower she relaxed as the warm water ran over her face, her back, her body. She closed her eyes and cried.

CHAPTER 5

It was Tuesday, and the morning routine was all there again. Paul had already left for the office. He usually left by seven leaving Lea to deal with waking up the kids and getting them ready for school all by herself.

"Jenny, are you up yet?" Lea said as she grabbed her robe and slippers and rubbed her eyes on her way out of her room.

"Yes, Mum, I'm heading down for breakfast," Jenny said as she took the stairs two at a time. Her bus would be there between 7:20 and 7:30 so she needed to rush to get done on time.

"Lauren honey, it's time sleepy head," Lea said as she shook her daughter's elbow. She was all cuddled up in her pink bed, her fleece pajamas keeping her warm on this cool morning. "Hmm," Lauren said not willing to open her eyes.

"Let's go baby, we need to get ready," Lea said again as she pulled up the blinds and turned on the light in the room to help her girl wake up.

"Colin, how are you coming?" Lea said, as she knocked on the bathroom door. She could hear her son flushing the toilet. "Let's go, I'll be downstairs," she said yelling through the closed door.

"Down in a minute," Colin said turning on the faucet.

"I need to use the bathroom," whined Lauren knocking on the door insistently.

"Use the one downstairs!" Colin said refusing to open the door.

"Lauren, use my bathroom," Lea said from the first floor trying to avoid any quarreling among her children so early in the morning.

"Jenny, peanut butter and jelly or hard-boiled eggs?" Lea asked as she opened the three lunchboxes in front of her and started putting food in them. For the most part, she tried to send healthy food to school, but many times the lunchboxes came home untouched, which annoyed her, and from time to time she would give in and send foods the kids would eat… Pop-Tarts, flavored yogurts, Goldfish, anything packaged or boxed.

"Neither," Jenny answered not very helpfully. "Can I just have some fruit?" she pleaded as she finished her cereal and packed her bag. For a supposedly conscious eater she still had her daily bowl of Frosted Flakes or Fruit Loops in the morning.

"OK," Lea said acknowledging her daughter but ignoring her request. She packed a piece of fruit, a hard-boiled egg, some chips, and an oatmeal cookie she took from the freezer.

"Got to go. Bye, Mum," Jenny said as she ran out the door.

Within half an hour the house became magically engulfed in a bubble of silence. For the first ten minutes of every morning, once the kids left the house, Lea felt a sense of peace like no other time. She could then just sit and stare into space or sip her warm cup of coffee if she had had time to get one, amidst the chaos of getting her kids out the door.

It usually only lasted ten minutes as either the phone would start ringing or Missy their golden retriever would start begging for some food.

This morning was no different, as if orchestrated by a

magic emcee the phone rang within ten minutes of Lauren hopping on her bus.

"Hello," Lea said slowly, coming back from her brief mental rest.

"Hi Lea, I assume Lauren is off to school? John just got picked up," Kara said.

"Oh hi Kara, yes Lauren got picked up about ten minutes ago," Lea said recognizing her neighbor's voice.

"It's a beautiful day. Should we take the dogs for a walk?" Kara asked as Lea glanced down to find Missy looking up at her with begging eyes, almost guessing Lea's conversation.

"Sure, I think Missy heard you. She is looking at me as if to say, Can we, Can we?" Lea said with a smile, rubbing her dog's ear.

"OK, I'll be at your house in ten minutes and then maybe we can walk to the park," Kara suggested.

Lea agreed, and putting the receiver down, she ran up the stairs to throw on some pants and a sweatshirt. Her sneakers were kept by the back door so she put her hair up in a ponytail and grabbed a cap from the bin by the back door as she put on her sneakers and grabbed Missy's leash.

"It's warmer than I thought," she said to herself as

she stepped outside and took in the morning air. "Poor Lauren, I insisted on her wearing her winter jacket today, she is going to be too warm with it by midday," she thought as she closed the door behind her, making sure not to lock it—she did not want to carry house keys with her.

Lea met Kara as she approached her house, her chocolate lab pulling on his leash as soon as he saw Missy.

Their dogs were used to playing together, and they did well when the two mothers found time to take them for a walk.

"So how have you been? I don't think I've seen you since school started," Kara said as she hugged her friend, and the dogs led them down a side street to the park.

"I know, this year the beginning of school has been crazy. Not sure if it's because Colin started middle school or Jenny high school, but I feel we've had more open houses and teacher meetings than ever," Lea said as she adjusted her sunglasses to fit under her cap.

"I know, I feel the same way, I find that as the kids get older there is more work on our end. Luckily my kids are pretty independent and they only ask for help when they need me to get them materials for school projects or things like that. I don't need to be on top of them for their work, thank god," Kara said with a smile.

Her children were really nice kids and she and her husband Steve did an amazing job with them thought Lea.

"How do you do that? My kids are all over the place. Every other night we have a late-night drama where one of them will have forgotten to do an assignment or to study for a test. Sometimes they forget, other times it's me. The other day I completely forgot Lauren had asked me to get some stuff for her project and Paul ended up going after work to buy her a poster board. By the time it was all done Lauren went to bed way too late," Lea said sounding frustrated.

"I know sometimes it's too much," Kara said understanding her friend. "What I do is I usually keep a stack of school supplies in a closet so we are never stuck in the middle of an assignment. I keep poster boards, new markers, glue, and things like that so that I don't need to run out and buy stuff last minute," Kara explained.

"That's a good idea," Lea said as Kara handed her a bag to pick up after her dog. Lea had forgotten to bring a bag. "What times are you teaching these days," Lea asked as they continued or their walk, their dogs happily wagging their tails.

"I'm teaching Tuesday, Wednesday, and Thursday mornings from nine to ten-thirty," Kara said referring to her yoga schedule. She had been a yoga instructor for over ten years. Even through her pregnancies, Kara had been able to teach right until the end and then she would be back teaching within a couple weeks after the birth. She had had her four children with a local well-respected midwife that was known for minimum intervention during labor and delivery, allowing her patients to recover much faster than if they had been given an epidural or another kind of pain medication.

"I'm going to try to make it one of these days. I'm struggling with my weight. I have twenty extra pounds that I can't lose. I try to eat well and I am now working out with this trainer, but it feels like I'm stuck in this size forever," Lea said with sadness. Her weight issue was something that kept her from fully enjoying her life. No one would think that she had so much weight to lose, but she knew that in order to feel great and be healthy she needed to get the weight off.

"Have you tried green smoothies in the morning? Focus on eating the right food, not limiting what you eat. That's the best way to go. Choose non-packaged foods and fresh fruits and vegetables," Kara said going through a list of foods and citing their pluses and minuses.

"What is a green smoothie?" Lea asked as they reached the park and sat on a bench after letting their dogs run free, off their leashes. They were both old enough to not run away; Missy was eight and Kara's chocolate lab, Bruno, was nine, so while they had enough energy to play for a while they usually stayed close.

"I've started making green smoothies, and I guarantee they work better than coffee. You mix one banana, one lemon, one cucumber, some celery, and some green leaves (spinach or kale) and you blend it all together with enough water to make a drink. You can add coconut water and ice chips if you want it cold. You have to try it," Kara said watching her friend's expression of disgust as she listed the vegetables.

"Trust me, if you have that in the morning, not only will you not be hungry for a while, but you also won't need any caffeine," Kara added as Lea still kept her face of disgust at the prospect of having that strange combination for breakfast.

"Mark and I belong to this CSA and we get great produce," Kara continued as she kept an eye on Bruno who was now playing with some other dog that showed up at the park.

"What's a CSA?" Lea asked. It seemed like her friend had all the answers this morning. Maybe more than she wanted to know.

"It's a community farming program. You buy a share at the beginning of the season and then every week you go and pick up your fresh produce, mostly vegetables. It's pretty cool because you know that what you are eating has been grown right there where you pick it. It also forces you to experiment with a lot of new vegetables you would never buy on your own. The kids are now eating all kinds of new things that I would never have known to buy had it not been for this program," Kara said getting her leash and heading to get Bruno as Lea leashed up Missy to begin their walk back home.

"That's cool," Lea said wondering if she would get her family to eat anything new. Plain broccoli was already a struggle. She suspected that having her children agree to new vegetables would be like feeding fish to a cow.

Kara continued explaining all the benefits of the CSA and the green smoothie and how Lea should try the smoothie for at least a full week before ruling it out. She also suggested that Lea come to her yoga class, which would help her relax and enjoy being in her body.

"I don't know," Lea said trying to take in her friend's suggestions in smaller doses. "I'll look at my schedule for the next few weeks and see if I can make it at least once or twice a week," Lea said, knowing that the truth was that there was not much going on in her schedule.

"Speaking of. There is a yoga/healthy living retreat in Costa Rica in November. I've been thinking of going. I checked the other day and they still have room. Do you want to come? It's the week before Thanksgiving."

"Not sure, I would have to check with Paul. Not sure if he can handle the kids' schedule," said Lea while thinking that it might be a good change for her but at the same time not thinking it would be possible.

"OK, talk to Paul about it. It's not too expensive and if you have miles you can buy the ticket that way. I'll call them this afternoon and get more information and then we can talk about it, all right? I really think that a change of air would be great for you, just what the doctor ordered," Kara said with a smile as she hugged Lea and walked into her house.

Lea walked the two blocks to her house considering the idea of going away for a whole week without her husband and the kids. She could not remember if she had ever done that since the babies were born or since she and Paul had married for that matter.

By the time she reached her house the dream had taken root in her mind and she could feel the beginning of a possibility.

It might actually be good for me, she said to herself as she walked into her house to face unmade beds, laundry that needed folding, dirty breakfast dishes, and a minivan that desperately needed vacuuming.

CHAPTER 6

The morning chaos had passed and Lea hopped in the shower after straightening the kitchen, starting a load of laundry, and making beds. She and her husband had given up in their attempts at having their kids do chores. They had gone over and over about it with them but to that day, their fifteen-year-old daughter was not capable of making her own bed in the morning nor picking up her clothes from the floor and putting them in the hamper in the bathroom, so Lea went room-by-room making beds and straightening up after her children.

"Leave their beds unmade and their clothes on the

floor. They'll learn their lesson that way," her mother-in-law would say as the expert who had raised wonderfully helpful children.

"I know, I know, I just can't stand the sight of the house a complete mess every day," Lea acknowledged that the problem was not her children but herself. She just couldn't stand the mess. Her cleaning up after them was probably the worst thing to do if she wanted them to take care of their rooms.

Halloween had come and gone and there was candy all over the house. The kids had dressed up with old costumes that were kept in a large basket in the playroom. Lauren had chosen to wear a ballerina costume that used to be Jenny's. The other two children had just thrown on black clothing, black hats, and black capes. With a mixture of cornstarch and food coloring they had smeared a blood-looking paste all over their faces and hands, in this witch meets Frankenstein, meets zombie costume.

It had been a warm night, Halloween night, but now November 4th the weather had finally changed and cold mornings no loner gave way to warm afternoons. Days were getting shorter and shorter and Lea had turned on the heat in the house.

As she finished her shower and pulled on some well-loved jeans and a handmade oatmeal-colored turtleneck, a Christmas gift that her mother-in-law had knit for her, she walked into her oldest daughter's room and opened the closet doors.

She did a mental inventory of Jenny's winter clothes and then wrote down in a pad what she needed to get for her. Jenny had grown three inches in the last year, and at 5' 6" and 120 pounds, she was no longer a girl. She probably was as tall as she would ever be, considering that girls usually stop growing at age fifteen or sixteen. Her pants were too short, her winter coat, new from last year, was too small already. She had squeezed into a girl's size sixteen last winter, but this year she was definitely a woman's small.

"Pants, coat, sweater, long-sleeve shirts, boots, sneakers," Lea wrote on her pad . . . the list was endless. She had planned her day to do errands, and while she knew she would not complete everything on her list she would at least go to the mall and get the basics. Another day she would take Jenny with her to finish up the rest.

Pulling some socks from her drawer, she went down to the kitchen to finish her shopping list.

Opening the fridge she wrote down what groceries she needed for the week. "Milk, yogurt, bread, ham and cheese, greens, ground turkey, pasta."

From the closet by the main door she grabbed her winter coat; it was the first day that she felt like she needed one. Temperatures were in the low forties. A warm October had given way to a sudden winter.

Lea pushed her shopping cart through the store. She had her list with her but as it always happened, halfway through her shopping run, she realized her cart kept filling up with items that were not on her list. Into the cart went Pop-Tarts, because they were on sale, Oreo cookies that her husband liked, but running through her mind were the conversations with her trainer and her yoga friend.

"Don't eat any processed food, try to stay with fruits and vegetables, whole grains," Kara had said on their last walk.

"Get some sugar-free Jell-O and low-fat ice cream, treats for when you are craving something sweet," had suggested the trainer.

Lea did not know what she should be eating, but she knew enough by now that fake sugars or packaged food were not the best for her or her family. She worried that unless she bought everything fat free and sugar free; she would never lose the weight.

She loaded the groceries into the car and headed to the mall. For Wednesday midday, the mall was quite busy. She walked straight to Old Navy and the Gap, where she knew she could find some of the basics on her list.

She looked through the winter coats at the Gap and found a couple that she liked. She couldn't believe she was now shopping for her daughter in the women's section! She went back and forth between two coats wondering which one would be the best choice for Jenny. She knew that there was a high chance that whatever she bought might need to be returned, but she made her choice and bought it.

Jenny had begun having an opinion about what she wanted to wear from a young age—she was probably as young as Lauren, eight or maybe nine, when she started fussing about what she would and would not wear. For a whole year she refused to wear skirts or dresses. Apparently, when she was in second grade, a boy in her class had commented that he could see her underwear when Jenny, in her dress, had sat on the floor with legs crossed during circle time. That comment from her classmate had embarrassed her so much that it would take a whole year for her to agree to wear anything but pants.

Lea was not much of a shopper. As the youngest of her siblings, she had always gotten hand-me-downs. Her two older sisters, one two years older, the other four years older, had chosen the outfits she wore most of her life ... until her first paycheck. While she did not love shopping, she had an eye for fashion and even though she regretted her current size, she always looked put together, with a simple but elegant look.

Like her, Jenny also did not love big frills. She was at that awkward age where she wanted to look like her friends, buying what was in fashion, which resulted in some mismatched outfits that did not always work well for her. She had always been a shy girl, not wanting to stand out too much; she avoiding being underdressed or overdressed.

Lea's mother had been a stay-at-home mum, just like her. She liked to sew, something Lea had never been good at, and Lea's childhood closet had been filled with either hand-me-downs, or custom outfits her mother would create with her magical sewing machine. Those were the days when there was not much discussion about what she would wear; her mother enjoyed dressing the three girls identically until her sisters were well into their teenage years. Thinking back and watching her daughter's rebellious teenage stage, Lea wondered how her sisters had put up with it. It had not been too bad for her; after all, she had only been twelve the last time she was out in public with her sisters in their identical party dresses, but her sister Susan had been fourteen and her sister Grace had been sixteen.

She remembered that last outfit. It was their holiday outfit for that season, and they wore it to their father's company Christmas party, as well as to their neighbors' parties and school events around the holidays. Considering that the three girls were now either young ladies or starting their puberty, the dress had a more adult look than the outfits they had worn before. Lea probably still had this dress in the attic. If she remembered correctly, her mother had kept the dresses for years. She then wrapped each one of them and gave them to her daughters.

The silk fabric had been soft to the touch, with beautiful handwork. Lea remembered the long nights when her mother had embroidered the three bodices with tiny pearls, a labor of love. The wide cream-colored skirt was cinched at the waist by a rose-pink velvet sash that tied in back with a small but tidy bow. The girls wore a petticoat with tulle under the dress to fill up the skirt. Her mum had gotten them three pairs of matching cream-colored flats with tiny pink bows in the front, and they each wore their matching dress winter coats with a set of gloves and hat to match. While Lea remembered her oldest sister's complaints, she also remembered the look of pride in her mother's eyes when the three girls, fully dressed and ready to go out, stepped down the long staircase, one after the other, perfectly poised, and recognizing their mother's love in the outfits. Her father had taken a picture of the three of them that particular night, the night of her father's Christmas party. Her mother still had that picture on her dresser.

Lea finished paying for her purchases and headed back to her car. It was two o'clock already and she was starving. She picked up a sandwich in the nearest drive through on her way home, not exactly what either her trainer or yoga friend had suggested.

"Thank you, Mum," Jenny said, coming down the stairs, after finding the outfits her mother had laid on her bed for her.

"You are welcome. Why don't you try everything on and we can see what works?" Lea said as she finished emptying the kids' lunchboxes and loading the dishwasher. Every afternoon brought the same routine, lunchboxes, homework, and after-school activities.

"Mum, I got an A on my project!" Lauren said running to her mother. She then washed her hands and climbed onto a stool by the counter to have her afternoon snack.

"Good job!" Lea said lifting her eyes to smile at her daughter. Lea leaned against the kitchen counter reading a pile of papers her son Colin had dropped on the counter for her on his way up to his room.

"Colin, can you come down please?" she called from the bottom of the stairs.

"One second," Colin yelled back from his bedroom.

"Not one second, now!" she yelled back.

"What?" Colin asked as he came into the kitchen.

"What? What do you mean by what? Can you explain this?" Lea said waving a math test in front of her son. The word FAILED appeared in bright red at the top of the page. "What happened here?" Lea asked.

"Nothing," Colin said shrugging his shoulders and walking past his mother to grab a cereal bar from the snack bin.

"Not nothing, this is something," Lea said not letting the subject drop; she moved over to stand right in front of her son.

"It's not a big deal. We were in the middle of a test and Max, who sits next to me, was struggling with the answers so he looked at me for help. I didn't say anything, I just moved my paper closer to him so he could see it," Colin explained.

"Did the teacher catch the two of you cheating? It takes two to cheat, you know that, right?" Lea said making sure she was clear on this.

Avoiding eye contact, he muttered, "Yeah, Max leaned over a bit too much, and the teacher caught him. He got slammed with a detention. The witch took the exam away from me and I couldn't finish. The hammer almost fell on me as well, but Max pleaded with the teacher and explained it was all his fault."

"You were lucky and I'm glad Max was honest.

Cheating is not right and helping someone cheat can get you in a lot more trouble than it's worth," his mother continued as she grabbed a pen and signed the exam. All exams with scores under 60/100 had to be signed by the parents.

"Let this be the last time," she said as she handed him the test and organized the rest of the papers.

"Mum, look," Lea heard her oldest daughter yelling from the top of the stairs.

"Can I watch TV?" Lauren asked as she finished her snack. She had sat watching the whole interaction about the test, processing the information, and now that it was over, she was ready for another entertainment.

"Go take a shower and then you can watch some TV," Lea responded as she climbed the stairs to Jenny's room. It was early for showers but with the shorter days the kids were heading to bed earlier, especially Lauren.

"So, what do you think?" Jenny asked as Lea walked into her room. Jenny was wearing her new coat.

"Do you like it? Is it comfortable?" Lea asked hoping for a yes. She did not have time in the next few days to exchange the coat and it was getting colder every day.

"Yes, it works," Jenny, said shrugging her shoulders.

"No, *it works*. Are you going to wear it?" Lea insisted.

"I guess so," Jenny answered. Lea knew that translated into a *Yes, I'll wear it*, these days.

"Great, then try on those tops and the jeans. The jeans I think you will love. They are supposed to look like skinny jeans but be a lot more comfortable," Lea said grabbing a pair of jeans and showing them to her daughter. She did not say that she had gotten a pair for herself—that would have made her daughter discard them instantly.

"I know. Mary has these, and she says they are really comfortable," Jenny said taking the jeans to the bathroom to try them on.

"I'll start taking stuff out of your closet," Lea said as her daughter left the room.

Lea began piling sweaters, tops, jeans, summer shirts, skirts, and bathing suits on top of her daughter's bed and put aside anything that was smaller than a girl's size 16 or a small adult.

As she emptied her daughter's pajama and underwear drawer to go through that, a little red box fell on the floor from Lea's overfilled arms.

She bent down to grab it as her daughter walked in the room and without hesitating she just stuffed it in her sweatshirt pocket, not sure why.

"Oh Mum. Do we have to do this now? I have a lot of homework to do and I was chatting with Lily," Jenny complained seeing the mountain of clothes on her bed.

"Let's do this quick. I bet you most of these clothes don't even fit you. If you want me to get you a few outfits before it gets too cold, we need to figure out what else you need," Lea said quickly grabbing a pile and inspecting her daughter's clothes. She sorted the clothes into a give-away pile, a Lauren future pile, and a "can't even pass it down pile."

Jenny reluctantly helped her mother and within thirty minutes they had sorted her clothes, to realize they needed to do a lot more shopping than what Lea had done that day.

"Maybe we can plan to go to Providence or even Boston on Saturday to get some more clothes," Lea said hoping that she would agree. It was hard to pin Jenny down for anything these days, especially if it involved time with her mother.

"Maybe," she said going back to her desk, her right foot under her as she seated herself in front of her computer. She was out of reach as soon as her fingers began flying over the keyboard. She was typing as fast as only kids her age can type these days chatting with two or three friends at a time.

"Make sure you finish your work before seven. Nana and Papa are coming for dinner tonight before they head to Florida next week," Lea reminded her daughter as she stuffed the piles of clothes into trash bags and lugged them downstairs.

Her in-laws had said, "Something simple. So we can see the kids before we leave," It was hard for them to see the kids on weekends, since there were so many activities that the kids were participating in.

Paul had agreed to come home early that night and Lea had canceled the kids' piano lessons so, for a change, all three kids were home from school and not going anywhere.

The days were getting shorter and by four o'clock in the afternoon, you could see the sun begin to set over the trees in the backyard.

Lea had put together lasagna that was ready to bake, and she was planning on a salad. Her mother-in-law was bringing dessert. Dinner was under control; Colin was in his room, Jenny was chatting with her friends, and Lauren had taken her shower and was watching TV in the playroom. With everyone engaged in their own worlds, Lea took the opportunity and went into her office and closed the door.

Sitting at her desk, Lea pulled from her pocket the

little box she had picked up in Jenny's room. She had never done anything like that, hiding something from anyone, but this time she had a feeling she needed to.

It was a small red box, the size of a matchbox, the kind that you used to get in restaurants everywhere. Nothing was printed on either side, but someone had written with a Sharpie in small well-rounded letters "For Jenny, XX00."

Lea slid open the box and inside she found a wrapped condom, a generic brand, nothing particular about it. With shaky hands Lea closed the box and put it back in her pocket. She was puzzled. She wondered if her daughter was seeing someone. Maybe she had a steady boyfriend she didn't know about? Maybe she should have been more involved in her daughter's social life? Her mind was racing at 100 miles per hour. Jenny was her oldest daughter so she had yet to experience parenting an almost adult woman.

Missy began scratching the door of her office with her paw and whining asking for her dinner. Lea turned off the light on her desk and walked back to the kitchen. "Now is not the time to deal with this," she said to herself as she turned on the oven up to 350 degrees to finish baking her lasagna. Missy waited patiently while Lea got a scoop of dog food and poured it into Missy's bowl. The golden retriever wagged her tail in expectation.

Grabbing a pair of scissors she walked outside to see if she could find anything that resembled a flower or something with which to put together a flower arrangement for the dining room table. She always liked to have some color on her table when she hosted dinner, even if it was just family.

She arranged a few purplish-brown hydrangeas in a vase that she would use as a centerpiece. She selected a tablecloth, pulled a pile of plates from the cupboard, and set the table for dinner. She would talk to Paul first and then, together they would sit down with Jenny and have a conversation; she put the issue aside for now.

CHAPTER 7

"*Hola,* Lea?" came the voice of Lea's friend Sonia as she slid the bar of her iPhone and picked up the call. It was Friday morning, the kids were off to school and she was driving to the gym, running late as always.

"Hi Sonia, how are you?" Lea said recognizing her friend's voice. The caller ID was blocked, as it was an international number.

"I'm doing well, how are you, the kids, Paul?" Sonia asked her accented English reminding Lea of her exotic friend.

"We are doing well. Everyone is getting so big, and they are all doing well in school," Lea answered vaguely as she tried to remember the last time they had spoken.

They used to talk almost every other week when they finished college. Sonia had come up from Argentina, her country of birth, to study in the US. They had been roommates for the whole four years, developing a sister-like bond that had kept them in touch all these years. Once done with college, Sonia had gone back to Buenos Aires, and after a few years she had married her long-time Uruguayan boyfriend Francisco Mendez, a polo player and financial investor. They spent their summers on the coast in a luxurious home in Punta del Este, a hot summer spot for Argentineans and Europeans. During the school year they lived in a large duplex apartment in Recoleta, Buenos Aires, while the kids went to school.

Lea was at Sonia's wedding, pregnant with Jenny at the time. She and Paul had flown down to Montevideo and then had rented a car to drive to Punta del Este where the event took place. It had been January 1996 and most of the out-of-town guests had stayed in one of the two five-star resorts in the area.

She remembered it as a week of party after party where beautiful women and well-dressed men danced until dawn. Good food, good wine, and amazing flowers were everywhere.

Sonia's dad was a powerful businessman in the oil industry. He had started with one or two oil rigs in Argentina and now owned multiple sites around the world bringing in billions of dollars every year.

Sonia was the only girl in a house with four children and as so, the most spoiled. Everything she wanted she had. The wedding itself was one of a kind, with over six hundred guests and live bands playing all night long. Her friend had been a queen in the clouds.

Lea remembered Sonia's wedding day as her friend talked. A custom-made Valentino gown that had been flown in from Italy accentuated Sonia's long body and blond hair. Sonia had gone twice to Italy for the fittings. On one trip she had invited Lea to join her, and they had spent a wonderful week in Venice.

The wedding itself had been a one of a kind experience for Lea. Luxury cars had been lined up for miles as the impressive list of guests showed up for the ceremony. Even the small local airport had been packed with activity as private jets landed day after day before the big event.

Lea and Paul had been treated as royalty. They did not have, at the time, being newly married and with a baby on the way, the financial means to attend the wedding; however, Sonia and her family had insisted on paying for their trip. Lea had felt embarrassed but she knew that she wanted to be there for her friend, and Sonia would hear nothing of Lea paying her back.

"That's great," Sonia said with her upbeat voice, bringing Lea back to the present moment and refocusing her mind on the conversation and the road ahead. Lea could picture her friend with her long blond hair pulled back in a ponytail, well put together, even if she was heading out for a run. She was not one to wear much makeup, and she always looked impeccably elegant.

"Are you in Buenos Aires?" Lea asked thinking that the weather should be getting warmer down there as the leaves finished falling around her house.

"No, I'm in Punta del Este," Sonia said, "Francisco and I came for the weekend to open up the house and get everything ready for the summer. We decided to host our whole family here for the Christmas holidays, so there's a lot to do. The kids stayed in Buenos Aires," she said taking a breath. "Sofia had a school event on Friday night, and the boys just wanted to hang out at home. Anyway I don't think Francisco invited them. He said he wanted to *whisk me away*—his words, — Sonia said with laughter in her voice.

"That's great, I wish Paul would *whisk ME away*," Lea said more to herself than to her friend.

"Are you guys OK?" Sonia asked quickly. "Anything going on?"

"We are fine, it's just I don't know … I'm a little lost right now … not sure why, but I don't know what to do with myself. I've been thinking that maybe I need to get a job, something creative, I don't know," Lea said while her friend listened. Their relationship had always been this way. Even if they did not speak for months, the moment they connected it never took them long to go deep into topics that each of them would bring up. Each would soon know if either the other one was struggling with something.

"I think you need a vacation, that's what I think," Sonia said resolutely. "Why don't we go somewhere," she added.

"Well, as a matter of fact, I have a local friend that is suggesting we go to a yoga retreat in Costa Rica. I'm not sure about that; I like yoga but not sure I like it that much, but maybe … it might be good," Lea said as she parked the car in front of her gym. She checked the clock on the dashboard and to her surprise she was five minutes early to her scheduled appointment with her trainer.

"Yoga retreat? Can we just go shopping somewhere instead?" Sonia asked jokingly.

"I know, it's probably not your thing," Lea said

knowing that Sonia was used to luxury resorts, first-class tickets, and *Leading Hotels of the World* destinations in Europe. If she remembered correctly her friend's honeymoon had involved a safari in Africa, a stay at Hotel Danieli in Venice, and a week in Rome.

"It might be fun though. When is this retreat? I could join you if it's before December. We are all coming to Punta del Este on December 15th to spend the holidays and the month of January, so if you are thinking November I might be able to do it." Sonia moved right into scheduling mode even if Lea had barely begun thinking of the possibility of taking the time and spending the money. Lea knew her friend well— if there was an opportunity to travel, Sonia was there. She rarely said no to an adventure.

"It's the second week of November, so it's coming up soon," Lea said wondering if she had lost her mind. She had never taken time away for herself since the children were born, let alone spend money on a trip. She had yet to even talk about it with Paul.

"I'm in. Send me an email with the where and when, and I can have Francisco's secretary get tickets, et cetera. I've never been to Costa Rica, but I've heard it's beautiful. What I can do is go to the retreat for a week via Miami, and then on the way back I'll spend a couple of days in Miami doing some Christmas shopping. That would actually be perfect. My mother will be around to keep an eye on the kids, but I have enough help here and they can handle them while I'm gone," Sonia continued. Lea wondered if she was talking to her or to herself. It amazed her how fast Sonia could make this kind of decision without even a hint of concern about money, childcare, or time.

"OK," Lea said a little overwhelmed by her friend's quickness. "Let me talk to Paul about it and then I'll let you know. I haven't even mentioned it to him yet," Lea said thinking over the evening's schedule and wondering if this would be a good time to bring it up.

"Do so, and if he has any issues about your going, let me know and I'll talk to him myself. After all, you work so hard with the kids and the house; you are always working, not sure how you do it all," Sonia said in support of her friend.

"And anyways it's high time we got together. I haven't seen you since last year when we met up in New York. And that was all of us together. It was good for the kids and all, but I want some time with you, so we can catch up and hang out like old times," she continued.

"OK, I'll talk to Kara my friend and to Paul and I'll let you know. I think he's going to be OK with it. We are not hosting Thanksgiving this year, and the kids don't have much going on that week so it should work out," Lea said as she got out of the car now running behind for her scheduled training appointment.

"Perfect. Call me on my cell, as I will still be here in Punta del Este until Sunday night. We came with some friends in their jet so we are pretty flexible on our return schedule which is great," Sonia added naturally, as if friends with private planes happened every day.

"Will do, gotta go now. Have fun and enjoy the time with Francisco," Lea said a little jealous of her friend in her weekend getaway.

"I should go away with Paul one of these days," she thought to herself as she climbed up the steps to the gym and met her trainer who was waiting for her at the door.

"Not late yet," Lea said with a smile pointing at the clock on the wall that marked ten o'clock.

"No, but almost," her trainer said with a grin as they walked toward the treadmill for the warm-up.

*

It was Friday night and the kids were finally in bed. It had been a good night and for a change they had all agreed on a family movie and had enjoyed watching it while eating their homemade pizza on the family couch.

"So what was it that you wanted to talk about?" Paul asked inviting conversation as Lea changed into her nightgown and brushed her teeth.

It was eleven o'clock by now and she was tired.

"I talked to Sonia today," she started as she loosened her ponytail and shook her head on the way to bed, her thick black hair falling over her shoulders. She slept on the left side of the bed, the side closer to the door.

"How is Sonia these days? Anything new and exciting?" Paul asked as he changed into his pajama bottoms, his bare chest still sporting a slim, toned torso. He did not work out much at all, but he still had a toned upper body with his upper arms showing the slight curve of his biceps.

"She is doing well. She and Francisco were in Punta del Este getting their house ready for the summer and taking some time alone, away from the kids," Lea said as she covered herself with the blankets and arranged her pillows.

"That sounds like the life to have… Should we go open our summer house and get some time away from the kids?" Paul said teasing her and inching himself closer to his wife.

He had not lost his desire for her, even through the years; it was Lea who had lost her drive these days. It was nothing to do with love; she just didn't feel like much more than a sweet kiss here or there.

"Sure," she said continuing with the joke.

"So is she taking you on an adventure?" Paul asked intuitively as always.

"Well, sort of. I walked with Kara the other day and she mentioned this yoga retreat in Costa Rica that she is going to. She wants me to go. It sounds like a good opportunity and now Sonia wants to go too.

"Yoga retreat, hmm? What do they do in a yoga retreat? Ommmmmmm all day?" he said sitting cross-legged on the bed mimicking a yoga pose.

"Stop it. You are going to wake up the kids," Lea said smacking him gently with the side of her *Simple Life* magazine that she had brought to read in bed. She was playing with him and it felt good. They had not had a light conversation in quite some time and she felt herself relaxing into it.

"When is it?" he asked as he responded to her smile and slid under the covers next to her, his head resting on his hand as he lay on his side looking at her.

"It's the week before Thanksgiving," she said, her body responding to his closeness, She too lay on her side facing him.

"Well go, then," Paul said without hesitation as he stretched his neck and kissed her nose. "But I'll miss you," he said as he put his hand on her hip.

"Really?" Lea said surprised. He was usually much harder to convince. He would always argue the kids' schedule or money issues ...

"No seriously, I think you should go. I know you have been struggling lately and I'm not sure why. Not sure if it's your midlife crisis or what, but I think you need a break and we'll be fine. I can handle the kids," Paul said lying back down next to his wife.

Even though they had lost each other a little bit lately, he had always been a good supporting partner. Lea could again find her old love in her husband that night.

"You are a nice guy," she said lifting herself on her elbow and kissing his nose.

"Yes, I am," he said locking his lips with her.

She responded to his touch as he lay on top of her, kissing her tenderly. Lea relaxed into his passion for the first time in a long time.

CHAPTER 8

It was Saturday morning and the house was quiet. For years, Lea remembered wishing for a sleep-in weekend, when the babies were young and never getting it. Now with two teenagers and Lauren much older, she and Paul got to have quiet mornings every weekend.

Paul woke up first and picked up his iPad that was never far from him and silently read the morning news, his finger swiping the pages as the light filled the room.

They both enjoyed morning and they did not close

their shutters at night; they welcomed the sun into their bedroom.

Lea stretched in bed, opened one eye, caught a glimpse of the screen out of the corner of her eye, and turned around and snuggled on the other end of the bed, closing her eyes again and enjoying the knowledge that she did not need to get up or rush.

She felt relaxed and content. As she opened her eyes slowly, the conversation they had had the night before came back to her mind. It sank in that she was going away. For the first time she was going to take a whole week away from her family to focus on herself!

"Good morning," Paul said as Lea rolled over and smiled at him. "Isn't it nice that everyone is sleeping?" he said as he moved a strand of hair from her face. "Even Missy is back to sleep after I fed her and opened the door for her this morning."

"Hmm," Lea said lazily as Paul kissed her and got up to hit the shower.

Lea lay in bed, listening to the water running in the bathroom of their master bedroom in contrast with the silence of the rest of the house. She began making plans in her mind, a smile on her face at the thought of seeing Sonia and what would be her reaction when she introduced her to her friend Kara ... probably the one friend of hers that was a polar opposite of Sonia.

"So what was it that you wanted to talk about the other night, when my parents came over, regarding Jenny?" came the voice of her husband as he walked out of the bathroom. A white towel surrounded his waist, another one hung around his neck as he cleaned his ear with a Q-tip.

The master bedroom though not large was laid out well. The adjacent bathroom gave them the privacy they needed to shower and change in their own space. A walk-in closet separated the bedroom from the bathroom.

"As I was cleaning Jenny's bedroom the other day, emptying the closet and drawers as she has outgrown most of her clothes, I found this little box," Lea said rolling onto her side and reaching into her bedside table drawer.

"What is it?" Paul asked sitting on the edge of the bed and grabbing the little red box that read *For Jenny, XX00*.

"Open it," Lea encouraged.

"Well. It could mean one of two things. Either it's nothing or a proposition from a boyfriend, date, friend, or something," Paul said coolly as he slid open the little box.

"Are you not worried?" Lea asked now sitting up and wondering what was wrong with her husband.

"Not yet," Paul said. "I think we should talk to Jenny about it. After all she is sixteen, and I'm sure some of her friends are sexually active. I also think that the school is probably giving these away left and right just in case. They used to give them away when I was a junior in high school," Paul said matter-of-factly.

"Really?" Lea said surprised. "I went to an all girls Catholic school. There was not even a conversation about this stuff. I know some of my friends were experimenting by then, but you know Mum, she had the three of us on a very tight leash," Lea said referring to her two sisters and the Catholic upbringing they had had, growing up in Connecticut.

"Well, let's sit down with Jenny and have a grown-up conversation with her. Until then I wouldn't worry about it," Paul said as he gave the box back to Lea and walked into the closet to get dressed. It was now nine-thirty in the morning on a lazy Saturday, and they were planning on a walk on the beach.

They used to walk as a family every weekend, but as the kids got older it had gotten more and more complicated to coordinate everyone's schedule. This morning though, for a change, their three children were home. Lauren was up watching TV; she knew how to set it up herself and quietly watch a movie and not wake up her parents, The teenagers were fast asleep, but Paul was planning on dragging them out of bed by ten and take the whole family on a cold beach walk.

Lea thought about the conversation with her husband as she put on some workout pants and a T-shirt. She was not surprised at his coolness; after all he was the one that never worried until there was a confirmed reason to do so.

She pulled back her hair into her characteristic ponytail; she would shower after their walk as she was hoping to run a little bit as well, maybe just fifteen minutes. Her trainer had suggested that if she didn't have time for a long run, to just try squeezing in little runs every day.

She remembered her junior year and how by then everyone had been dating. They used to go to the movies in large groups of friends or to private parties where the parents of the hosting friend would be right there to watch them at all times. Lea remembered those days fondly. They had fun with each other in the innocence of that first love. Some of her friends talked about a little bit more than a kiss or holding hands, but Lea was for some reason too naïve to explore beyond that. She had been well into college before her steady boyfriend at the time suggested that they step up their relationship. That boyfriend had been Paul, so at age thirty-nine, she had had only had one partner in her life and she sometimes wondered if she was missing something. She had never thought much about it before, until the last few years, when sexual conversations with her girlfriends became more open than ever before.

"I remember my first boyfriend. He was great! We had a great physical relationship, but in the long run he could not commit to me," her friend Jessie had said one night at a girls night out. Lea had quite a few local friends that she had made since she and Paul moved to the area. They had all met through playgroup originally but they chose each other's company long after their babies had outgrown diapers and were well into school. Sometimes they would go out for dinner, but mostly they would just go out for walks while the kids were at school or sit together at the beach, even though the kids no longer wanted to join them.

"I had a couple of boyfriends before I met my husband, " her other friend Sarah had said. "Steve and I did not meet until I was done with school and we were both working full time in Miami. We were coworkers," she explained, referring to her now twenty-year marriage with her husband Steve.

"Lea, did you date much before you met Paul? I know you guys married young," her friends had asked her. Lea had been embarrassed for some reason to admit that in fact Paul had been her only lover, so her answer had been vague, not wanting to share much.

Now as a mother of a sixteen-year-old she was torn

between her upbringing and her feelings as an older, married woman. She worried about all the possible "dangers" of her daughter becoming sexually active: sexual diseases, disappointment, heartbreak and even pregnancy but at the same time she wanted her daughter to explore and grow as a woman. Maybe not at sixteen but soon. She also worried about sending her daughter off to college before it happened. She wanted to be there for her daughter when she decided to take that step with a partner, to support her,

"I called you last night and you were not home . . . it was late," her mother's voice came into her mind as Lea remembered those days, back in New York City, when she and Paul were dating and her mother would check in on her every evening.

With no cell phones at the time, it was easier for parents to check on their children. Her mother would call every evening at around nine-thirty to make sure her daughter was home in her rented two-bedroom apartment that she shared with a roommate. If for some reason her daughter was not home, then her mother proceeded to call every hour until 12:30 AM until she found her daughter. One night there was no answer; her daughter had not come home to sleep.

"I was with Paul. I stayed over," Lea had answered counting on the distance between them to protect her from her mother's reaction. She said it straight away, trying to sound confident and mature, but in truth her hands were shaking, her face was red, and she was sweating all over.

"I understand," had been the only words her mother could muster. "Is he committed to you? Are you engaged?" were her mother's next words.

"Mum, I'm twenty-one years old, legally an adult, and yes he is committed. He and I have been dating for the last year and no, we are not engaged," Lea had answered rolling her eyes at her mother as if she were sitting right in front of her.

Lea finished tying her sneakers as she heard the kids downstairs in the kitchen.

"So, should we all go for a walk?" she said as she kissed the top of Lauren's head and welcomed the warm mug of coffee her husband handed to her as she took a seat at the table. Bagels, cereals of all kinds, butter, jelly, jam, strawberries, bananas, frozen waffles, and even a couple of sunny side up eggs were randomly placed in the center of the table.

"Daddy and I made breakfast!" said Lauren with a smile as she sipped her chocolate milk and spread double layers of jelly on her toast.

"Yes, we did," said Paul with a smile.

"I have a lot of homework," Jenny said as she grabbed a couple of strawberries and ate them holding them by the stem. She was still wearing her pajamas, her blond hair loosely tied in a ponytail.

"We'll just be gone an hour. It's a beautiful day and we want to go as a family," Paul said not insisting but with a firm voice.

"It's too cold," whined Colin, who was now on his second serving of waffles and large cup of hot chocolate.

"Oh, don't be a chicken," teased Paul as he messed with Colin's hair, which was sticking up, as it usually was, when he woke up.

Indeed, it was a beautiful cold November day as they parked near the beach, the teenagers dressed and wearing multiple layers, Lauren happy to have the whole family out for a change. The air was crisp and clear with only a few clouds in the distance. Beautiful round waves were breaking on the hard cold sand.

The five of them wearing their winter jackets, hats, and gloves strolled down to the beach letting Missy follow them at her own pace. Lauren ran ahead flying a kite they had brought, and Colin, fully awake by then, ran behind her trying to get a turn. It was amazing how at his thirteen years of age he could sometimes act so mature and at other times seem like such a little boy.

"Jenny, can we talk?" Paul said walking up to Jenny

who was slowly walking by the shore, her UGG boots getting slightly wet as she played with the waves trying to walk as close as she could without getting soaking wet.

"Hmm?" Jenny answered looking up at her father and shrugging her shoulders.

Lea walked up to them and paced her step to walk on Jenny's other side. Missy kept up with the trio.

"Jenny, your mother found a little box in your room the other day. A little red box with a condom inside," Paul started as he put his hands in his pockets; he had forgotten his gloves.

"Mum, you were looking through my stuff?" Jenny said looking at her mother, her cheeks flushed, her eyes open wide.

"No honey, I wasn't, but the other day when we pulled out all your clothes to determine what no longer fit, this little box fell on the floor as I pulled your T-shirts from the drawer," Lea said pulling the little red box from her jacket pocket. She had brought it in case they had the opportunity to talk.

"It's nothing," Jenny said shrugging her shoulders. "We had a speaker come into the school last week, and they were talking about stuff, that kind of stuff," Jenny said vaguely.

"Yes?" Paul said patiently encouraging his daughter to continue.

"I think the woman was a doctor, or something like that. Anyway, they separated boys from girls and put senior and junior year girls together for the talk. She was just talking about pregnancy, diseases, that kind of stuff, and how to be responsible and the consequences."

"Anyway, McKenzie was sitting next to me, and you know how she likes to joke around. She decided to dedicate my sample to me and so she did, no big deal," Jenny said still a little bit annoyed that she was having to explain all this stuff to her parents.

"You know you can always talk to us, right? If you ever have any questions, please make sure to ask us. We can help you," Lea said putting her arm through her daughter's in a gesture of closeness and friendship.

"Sure Mum, I know," Jenny said stiffening up at her mother's touch. Lea knew her daughter felt uncomfortable when Lea approached her these days. Gone were the times when Jenny, as a little girl, would run to her mother's lap. Nowadays she could barely get a wave good-bye when Lea dropped her off at a school event or even a friend's house.

"Can I go now? I want to get a turn with the kite?"

Jenny asked her parents hoping the conversation was over.

"Sure, go ahead," her father, said as Jenny ran ahead and Paul locked arms with his wife as they walked down the beach.

"I told you it was nothing," Paul said with satisfaction in his voice.

"I know, I hope she is telling the truth," Lea said somehow praying the whole thing was as simple as this.

"Oh, she is. Look at her playing with Lauren and Colin; she doesn't look older than twelve right now," Paul said watching his children play in the distance.

"I can't believe they are already that big," Lea said in a whisper, her hopes for a run growing dim. She felt comfortable walking with her husband; she enjoyed connecting with him while watching her three children play like old times. She felt content, recognizing the joy in her family. A joy she many times forgot was there.

CHAPTER 9

Lea added the last few things to her suitcase and went downstairs.

"Here's a list of meals that are in the fridge ready to heat," she said putting a printed-paper in front of her husband who was sipping his coffee.

"Here's the kids' schedule and when Karla is coming to help out. Please make sure you leave the door open for her; she doesn't have a key and doesn't want one either," Lea continued placing another piece of paper in front of her husband who now had no choice but to put down his newspaper.

"Lea, it's only seven in the morning. You are not leaving until noon," Paul reminded her as he grabbed a piece of toast and began spreading margarine and jelly on top.

"I know, but you will be leaving in twenty minutes and I won't see you again," she said to her husband recognizing that she was maybe overdoing it a bit.

"Not ever again, I'll see you in about a week. Part of the deal of you going is that you have to come back home to us, remember?" Paul teased her as he stood up and kissed her on her forehead before heading up the stairs to brush his teeth and get going to work.

"Of course I will," Lea responded now running around the kitchen getting lunchboxes ready. "Don't forget when you do the lunchboxes to make sure that they each get a fruit every day," Lea said to her husband as he waved his hands in the air like saying "whatever" and left her speaking to herself in the kitchen.

"I love you, and be safe," Paul said to his wife as he came back through the kitchen on his way out the door.

"I will," she said turning around to kiss him, his arms coming around her as he lightly touched her lips. "Thank you for giving me this time," she said acknowledging her privilege and thankful for it.

"You deserve it," he said as he grabbed his newspapers and walked out.

"OK guys, let's move it. It's almost 7:20. Jenny, the bus will be here any second now," Lea said yelling from the bottom of the stairs as soon as she heard her husband's car pull out of their driveway and drive away.

"I'm coming," said Jenny with a sleepy voice.

Lea finished the lunchboxes, grabbed a breakfast bar from the pantry, and handed it to her daughter as she came down too late to sit down for breakfast.

"Jenny, please be good this week, help Daddy when you can, and be good at school," Lea said kissing her daughter on her forehead and reminding her of her big-girl responsibilities while she was gone.

"Colin, Laruen, let's go," Lea said as she hurried around the kitchen cleaning up and loading the dishwasher trying to leave the house as clean as possible before heading to the airport.

Colin's bus came as he was putting on his shoes and he ran for it with one shoe on, one shoe off.

"I love you, see you in a week," Lea managed to say as she saw him to the door.

"OK, Lauren, you now have five minutes," she said turning around to her elementary school girl and the third bus schedule.

"I love you, Mum. I'll miss you," said Lauren as she hugged her mother tightly and ran out the door when they saw the bus turn the corner.

Lea closed the door behind her youngest daughter and took a deep breath. It was now 7:45 AM. She had two hours to get out the door for their noon flight. She was scheduled to pick up Kara and they would drive Lea's car to Logan Airport. Sharing the cost of parking made more sense than hiring a limo to drive them and that way they had more control over their schedule and no risk of not being picked up on time upon their return.

Lea walked back to the kitchen and finished loading the last few breakfast bowls into the dishwasher, switched loads of laundry, and grabbed her now half-empty cup of coffee. She brought the coffee upstairs with her while she checked the kids' rooms. All of them had made pitiful attempts at making their beds. Jenny's room had clothes all over, while Colin had left his dirty soccer uniform on his bedroom rug, mud from his socks everywhere.

Lauren room's was probably the cleanest of them all even though her stuffed animals had remained all over the floor after Lauren kicked them out of her bed in the middle of the night.

Lea looked at the clock on the wall and gave herself twenty minutes to quickly run through each room and straighten it up. She knew she shouldn't if she wanted them to learn to take care of their belongings. Her mother had reminded her many times.

"If you want the kids to be responsible for their things, having a "fairy godmother" come and straighten up their stuff while they are at school will not help. They will expect this "fairy godmother" the rest of their lives," her mother would remind Lea over and over again when Lea complained.

But she was going away for a week and there was a little bit of guilt in her, so she cleaned up as best as she could in the little time she had before hopping into the shower.

Her bag was mostly packed and as she finished her shower she made a mental inventory of her suitcase.

Yoga pants and tops had been the first items to be packed, two of them as a matter of fact. She actually had to buy some new ones, as what she usually wore for yoga were very old workout pants and old T-shirts that she would be embarrassed for anyone to see outside of the small group of women that attended yoga in the studio nearby. She had also packed one bathing suit, a two-piece tankini, which covered enough of her trouble spots for Lea to dare wear it in public. She also had a pair of jeans and a pair of black-cropped pants, sandals, sneakers, and one pair of black high-heeled sandals in case they had a night out. She had packed a simple black dress and a silver shawl. She was hoping for at least one dress-up night, where she could go out for dinner with the girls.

While Sonia had visited Lea in her current home, she had never met her friend Kara and Lea wondered how they would get along. Going away with two friends that were so opposite in personality could possibly be a wonderful experience or a miserable one. She was hoping the retreat would be engaging enough to keep the three of them in line.

Kara was the picture of the perfect all-natural organic mother, sometimes referred to as "crunchy granola," but there was nothing old fashioned or hippie about Kara. She was always well put together; her children were always well behaved and well dressed. Her home-cooked meals were nothing but mouth-watering delicious. Lea had sampled a few when Kara brought dinner for the family after Lauren was born, a gesture from her neighborhood friends that Lea still cherished and that she had reciprocated when Kara and other friends had had newborns.

Kara was enthusiastic and courageous and she had begun her yoga studio with a few classes here and there. Now she had a good amount of followers that participated in different classes and workshops, as Kara had opened the door for other teachers to teach and share their teaching with her students and the community.

She was humble about her achievements, but nevertheless recognized that what she had created out of nothing had become an important part of their community, something people valued and supported. Lea felt honored to be going to this retreat with Kara. While Kara attended many of these a year, this one she had decided to not advertise to all in the studio but to just go on her own with Lea.

It was 9:15 AM. Lea added her toiletries to her bag, and looked around her closet one more time. She zipped up the bag and brought it downstairs.

She was wearing a comfortable pair of jeans, a pair of black ballerina flats, a long-sleeved white shirt, with an orange silk scarf around her neck, and a safari-style cotton jacket. She knew she would be cold now but did not want to wear anything more, as it would be quite warm when they landed in Costa Rica.

With five minutes to spare she filled a reusable bottle with water and packed her new addition, a collapsible water bottle for her to take on the trip. She had learned the impact of bottled water in the environment from a project her son Colin had recently done at school. After learning that only 20% of bottled water bottles are recycled and that more than forty million bottles end up in the dump every year; Lea and her family had committed to reduce the amount of bottled water they consume.

Lea no longer bought those little bottles of water that she had thought were cute and convenient at one time. The kids now took to school reusable bottles filled at home that they would refill in bubblers throughout the day if needed.

Traveling internationally will prove another challenge in staying committed to using less bottled water, but Lea was willing to give it a try.

It was cold and gray but there was nothing in the forecast should affect their travel plans.

Right on time, Lea pulled out of her garage and out of their driveway on her way to Kara's house.

"Did you leave already?" Paul asked as Lea picked up her cell phone.

"Just did," Lea said.

"Well, have a good flight and call me if you can. You have your passport, right?" he asked as always, taking care of his wife.

"Yes I do, thank you. I'll call as soon as I can when we land and if I can't find a phone I'll just send you an email. I won't have my cell phone on as it will be very expensive to use down there," Lea said as she pulled into Kara's driveway.

"OK, I love you. Be safe and send my love to Sonia. Tell her to come visit us soon," Paul said, as Lea was about to get out of her car to ring the bell when Kara saw her through the window and waved that she was coming out.

"I love you too," Lea said as they ended their conversation.

"Ready?" Lea asked Kara as she got out of the car and helped her friend with her luggage.

"Yes!" Kara said lightly hugging her friend in the driveway before loading her bags and getting in the passenger seat, a big smile on her face.

"We have everything? Passports?" Kara asked fastening her seatbelt.

"Got it," Lea said as she reversed the car into the road.

"Then off we go," Kara said with a smile. "It feels so good to be going to a retreat when I am not running any of it," she said.

Kara used to do this kind of traveling all over the world before she and her husband had kids or even before she was even married, but in the last few years, with four kids, she ran many retreats, but rarely attended one as a participant.

"I'm so excited," Lea said looking at her friend. "I've

never left everyone for a whole week, I feel a little guilty though, but I wouldn't change it for anything! While Paul has always been supportive, I was so surprised he agreed to let me go with such short notice and for so long," Lea said still not believing that she was taking this time away all for herself.

"He's a nice guy and he loves you," Kara said almost reminding her friend of her own husband's virtues.

"He is," Lea said now thinking fondly of her partner.

The drive up to Boston was uneventful and they made it to the long-term parking lot in little over an hour. Traveling had become harder and harder in the last few years with exhaustive security checks and full planes that had taken away the fun and excitement of airplane travel that Lea remembered from her childhood.

"Do you remember when traveling was a whole adventure in itself, the airplane part?" Lea asked her friend as they unloaded the bags and wheeled them into the terminal. "My mother used to dress the three of us in fancy matching outfits whenever we went to Florida to see my grandparents. We would fly from New York and we would get a full meal, kids' goodie bags, and all kinds of special treats, " Lea said as they entered the terminal.

"I know, it was so much fun, the flight attendants

were all beautifully dressed. With their long legs and long blond hair, they all looked like Barbies," Kara said referring to the perfectly uniformed flight attendants of their childhood years. These days traveling, while still expensive, had become something so common that there was no magic to it.

Having done the check-in online at home, Kara and Lea only had to show their printed boarding passes to an agent that collected and tagged their luggage.

"So, when and where are we meeting your friend Sonia?" Kara asked as they stood in line at security check, now almost bag free, each of them carrying only a small carry-on bag.

"Sonia is flying to Miami right now—actually she should have landed this morning as she took the overnight flight from Buenos Aires. She wanted to go through Miami so that on the way back she can do some Christmas shopping and visit some friends," Lea explained as an agent stamped her boarding pass and she began the tedious process of taking off her jacket, scarf, and shoes and placing all her belonging in thick plastic gray bins on the stainless steel table that fed the conveyor belt feeding people's personal stuff through the scanner.

"You were smart wearing flats," Kara said pointing to Lea's now bare feet. Kara was wearing zip-up boots that were not as easy to get off. "I should have worn socks though," Lea said now feeling the cold marble dirty floor under her feet.

They were seated in their plane before long and they took off on time.

"So are you ready for this?" Kara asked Lea as the plane reached its cruising altitude and Kara was able to relax again. She did not say much about it but Lea had noticed the droplets of sweat on her friend's forehead and her white knuckles holding on to the seat's armrest as they were taking off and wondered if her yoga always calm friend was struggling with anxiety issues about flying.

"Were you nervous when we took off?" Lea said now bringing up the subject and wondering if there was something in Kara's past that would bring her this level of anxiety.

"Yes," Kara said with a shy smile. "I know it sounds weird but ever since I saw a plane crash soon after landing I have been having anxiety when flying. I try to control it and it was getting better. For a while, in my twenties, I was traveling everywhere. Lately, knowing that the kids are back home makes it harder for me to relax, I can't stop wondering what would happen if this time the plane really went down. Once the takeoff is over and we are cruising I'm usually OK as long as there is not much turbulence," she explained as she accepted a glass of water offered by the flight attendant.

"That is terrible. Where were you when you saw the plane? How old were you?" Lea asked her eyes wide, hungry for details.

"I'll tell you all about it when we get there safely," Kara said trying to not blow her friend off but not willing to engage in that kind of conversation.

"So, is this a really intense retreat? I'm worried that Sonia and I might not be mentally or physically prepared for it. We both needed an excuse for some time away from our families, any time away from our families," Lea said accepting a glass of water from the flight attendant and giving her credit card to get a beer as well.

"Well, there won't be much beer or wine," said Kara smiling as the flight attendant brought the beer to her friend.

Lea had a seat by the window and Kara was squished in the middle seat. A man in his forties sat next to Kara on the aisle seat browsing a brochure about Costa Rica.

"OK, no alcohol, I can deal with that. What else, yoga every day? All day? Any massages? Any pedicures?" Lea said half jokingly but hoping that there would be some pampering and not just hard work.

"I think, Lea, that if you are able to fully embrace the experience, this would be a wonderful week for you. You will be able to fully connect with yourself and with your body," Kara said somehow putting on her yoga master hat again and not just in the casual friend role.

"I'll try. I know I need to, but I also know that I'm fighting it. The last few months I could barely concentrate when I did show up for yoga class, and while I know I should be meditating, eating less sugar, and connecting with myself more, I find it hard, almost like I'm rebelling against it," Lea said now getting serious and truly voicing her concerns about this experience.

"That's your body fighting it because of fear; you have to let go, bring down your barriers and try to mindlessly while mindfully ease into the experience, any and all experiences, don't fight them," Kara said in a gentle voice.

"You noticed that I was struggling there when we were taking off, right? I was, I won't deny it. I had closed my eyes and was meditating to bring ease to my body through my mind. I was struggling, fear overcoming my efforts for mindful relaxation, but I stayed with it. I kept going even if you noticed me sweating or holding on to my chair. I still tried because I have no choice. Some people take medication or drink alcohol. I need to engage my mind to help me relax, otherwise I might end in a panic attack," Kara said opening up about her experience with her fear of flying.

"Fear is what blocks us from fully jumping in the pool, fully immersing ourselves in life, in relationships, in ourselves, in everything. Fear is what makes us live our lives as if we were wearing gloves, holding on to things, embracing our loved ones, but never really fully touching them, touching life," Kara said as she pulled out a brochure from her purse and handed it to Lea.

"Take a look at this, and you'll have a better understanding of where we are going, and what to expect, but keep your mind open to new adventures. Stay open to engaging in different experiences that will help you grow spiritually and physically. Even if I'm with you and Sonia is joining us, make this trip about you, not about us, and you'll be amazed how much more you can connect to us and other people in the retreat when you first focus on connecting with yourself. You will be able to open up from a familiar place, from a place of home, of strong standing and rooted feet," Kara said as she took out a book and opened it where marked, thus indicating that she was now looking for some quiet time.

They still had three hours to go out of the four-hour plane ride. Lea heard what Kara had said and she leaned her head against the window and stared into nothing as the plane cruised above the clouds.

She heard Kara's words about connecting with herself. She understood what she meant. Last week she and the kids had been watching some old home videos she found when cleaning up her bedroom bureau. There were videos from when Jenny was young, some of Colin, and then a few from when Lauren was born.

She was amazed and sad to see herself in those videos. She felt sadness for the time past and the days when her children were babies; she also felt sad that the things that bothered her then were still bugging her today, mostly her weight and her self-esteem around that. She watched a video where she was happily playing outside in the yard with her then two-year-old son. She was wearing a tank top and a skirt, and she seemed happy. Colin was laughing and playing around her, even hugging her, but she could see that her eyes were sad. She's the only one that would notice.

She recognized the sadness and she felt it now, but she couldn't explain it, either to herself or to people around her, to the point that she was embarrassed by it somehow. She had a good life, maybe even much more than many girls she knew growing up, but she still had a place within herself that was not completely happy. She knew connecting with herself was what she needed to do, but she feared it, probably as much or more than Kara's fear of flying.

Opening the brochure she focused on the pictures showing the beauty of the place where they would be staying, the wooden decks opening to luscious greenery, the waterfalls and beaches. She was going to take Kara's advice and focus first and foremost on herself, on finding pleasure through a journey into her core.

Landing was easier on Kara than Lea had expected. Within minutes they had claimed their bags and found themselves standing in the center of a whirlwind of activity. There were people everywhere, tanned, good-looking people wearing shorts and T-shirts or flowery dresses. There was a sense of ease and vacation. People were smiling, not rushing past you. In the middle of all this, Lea spotted her friend Sonia standing in the middle of her own whirlwind, looking lost.

Her blond hair and long red nails contrasted with the natural atmosphere in the small airport terminal; she had two large Louis Vuitton bags and a small carry-on. Her high-heel sandals gave her a few extra inches that she needed to wear her black maxi dress with style. Big silver loops glittered through her mane and her makeup was impeccable.

"She flew all night?" Kara asked speechless as they approached Lea's friend, not believing that someone could look so glamorous after spending the whole night on a plane.

"First class," Lea said smiling as she opened her arms to embrace her long-time friend.

"*Hola!*" greeted Sonia as she hugged and kissed her friend.

"Sonia, this is my friend Kara, Kara this is my friend Sonia," Lea said formally introducing her two friends.

"How are you?" Sonia said ignoring Kara's stretched-out hand and kissing her on the cheek, just one cheek, and taking Kara by surprise.

"Sorry, that's how we do it in Argentina, I forget I'm supposed to shake hands," Sonia said blushing, which made Kara feel a little bit better.

Kara was starting to feel that this trip might not be such a good idea after all, bringing along not only her not so sure friend Lea but also now this Vogue model look alike.

"Should we get a taxi?" Sonia asked in perfect English. A hint of a British accent gave her an air of sophistication that she was not even aware of.

"We should be picked up. Let's see if we can find the van," Kara said heading toward the exit door.

"Let me take one," Lea said smiling and helping Sonia

with her multiple bags. "I thought you were going to go shopping in Miami after the retreat. What's with all these bags?" Lea said as she rolled her own suitcase and her friend's toward the exit doors.

"Oh, you know me. I couldn't make up my mind, and I also have a few events to go to in Miami before I go home," Sonia explained as she click-clacked behind Lea.

"So, is this a serious retreat or are we allowed to have some fun?" Sonia asked as they reached the van and left their bags by the curb while they hopped in.

"Excuse me, are these your bags?" said a peaceful faced man in his thirties peeking his head into the van.

"Yes," said Sonia.

"OK, I'll get them in," the man said almost informing her that he was doing a favor more than his job.

"Thank you," Sonia smiled wondering why she felt like she was supposed to be grateful for his service, assuming he was part of the organizing team.

The three women took the seat in the last row as other passengers started climbing in the van.

The man who had helped them with their luggage took a seat in the middle row right in front of them. He was wearing linen sand-colored pants, leather sandals, and a white linen shirt hanging over his pants. He looked elegant yet comfortable and relaxed. His tan hinted of his way of life or at least the fact that he did not come from a cold part of the world.

"Good afternoon, everyone," said the driver turning around to face the van full of people.

"Welcome to Costa Rica and welcome to the Kalawi Yoga Center. We are now heading straight to the center where your guides will show you around and introduce you to the program. If you have any questions, please do not hesitate to ask," he said in English, British English to be more precise.

A blast of tropical air had hit them as they left the air-conditioned terminal. The van they soon discovered did not have air-conditioning. With twelve passengers it was hot in the van, so the windows were open bringing in the warm, humid air.

"It's hot in here," Sonia whispered to Lea as she nodded in agreement. As they left the airport they could see acres and acres of green land. Little narrow streets suggested that these were the entrance to houses buried behind trees and shrubs. To the naked eye, all you could see were walls of green vegetation.

"Let me introduce myself. My name is Alex von Bearb" said the helpful gentleman who had helped them with their bags. He was sitting in front of Lea and her friends, so he turned around and extended his hand. His hand was strong and big Lea noticed, and he also had an accented British English.

"My name is Lea, and these are my friends Sonia and Kara," Lea said as she sat in the middle and shook Mr. Von Bearb's strong tanned hand. "Nice to meet you," she continued now realizing that in fact this guy had indeed helped Sonia with her bags out of courtesy not because it was his job. *Good thing that Sonia didn't try to tip him; that would have been embarrassing,* she thought.

"Are you all from America?" he asked insisting in conversation. He had now turned his body, as much as he could, to face them.

"Kara and I are from Massachusetts, but Sonia is Argentinean and lives in Buenos Aires," Lea said pointing to her friend as Sonia smiled without committing to a conversation.

"I see, and are you looking forward to the retreat? I've been doing this retreat for years and it's incredible how every year I learn new things even though I know exactly what to expect. Is this your first time?" he asked making Lea a little bit uncomfortable with his attention, but at the same time enjoying it. He had a way of speaking peacefulness in his voice and in his face that she found fascinating and soothing at the same time.

"Yes, it's my first time. To be honest I'm not sure what to expect. I'm coming a little bit in the blind—maybe that's a good thing," Lea said shrugging her shoulders and smiling. "Where are you from?" she asked curious about his accent. He was obviously not originally from an English-speaking country.

"I'm Austrian, from Vienna, but I've been living everywhere in the last ten years," he answered.

"Your English is very good," Lea continued.

"I was brought up in a British boarding school outside of Vienna and as a young kid my sister and I always had British nannies so we grew up speaking English," he explained as the van pulled into a long palm tree lined driveway.

"Here we are," said the driver as he opened the doors.

The center was located on a hill, overlooking the ocean. The whole place was built in wood with beautifully polished floors everywhere that opened up to verandas with a view of the water.

The main entrance had the feeling of a minimalist lobby of a fancy hotel. Yoga blankets were spread everywhere for people to sit as were multicolored cushions and low wooden tables. The front desk, on the right side of the lobby as you entered the hotel, was bustling with energy as young people working the counter rushed in and out of a back office bringing papers, welcoming guests, and handing out information.

"Welcome to our Yoga Center," said a tall slim young girl approaching the three friends as they walked in. She was wearing a long orange tunic with a bright pink sash around her waist. A large wooden beaded necklace hung around her neck; her blond hair fell loosely to her shoulders.

She bowed with her hands clasped in front of her as she smiled at the three women.

"My name is Cielo and I will be your personal guide this week," she said introducing herself in perfect American English.

"Hello," said Lea and Sonia, while Kara bowed back to Cielo with her hands clasped in front of her, and whispered something Lea and Sonia could not hear.

"Please, here is where we leave our shoes. We do not wear shoes anywhere inside the center, only when we go outside," Cielo said pointing to cubbies disposed on each side of the main entrance where people had already been placing their shoes neatly in each space.

"I think I'll just take these with me. I don't think I'll wear them to go outside," said Sonia as she took off her high heels and stuffed them in the bag she was carrying.

"Let me help you with your luggage," Cielo offered Sonia as she struggled to grab all her stuff.

"Oh, thank you," Sonia said smiling back to Cielo. Lea could tell that her friend was feeling a little bit uncomfortable with her high heels, makeup, and long red nails.

"What does Cielo mean?" Lea asked as she walked ahead of her friends on the way to their rooms. "You sound American and the name does not sound familiar," she continued intrigued by her name.

"I am American, from Michigan, but I've been living in Costa Rica for the last five years. I came for a retreat and never left," Cielo said smiling. "My birth name is Lauren," she said as they walked past open rooms with people unpacking their belongings.

"Oh, my daughter is named Lauren; that's so funny. So who named you Cielo?" Lea said as they walked down another long corridor. They seemed to be going through long buildings, almost like long houses, with the rooms on their left as they walked away from the main building, all the rooms overlooking the ocean.

"When I decided to stay here and work in the community I was given a name that better fit my journey. Cielo means sky in Spanish, and I chose it because it is under the wide-open sky that we realize our smallness and our greatness. We realize that the bigger world around us holds us in its core, and we also recognize the greatness of ourselves in being able to open up our souls to that energy making us bigger than we are, and enabling us to energize the world from our small source," Cielo explained naturally. Lea puzzled about the deepness of her comments.

"Here you are," Cielo said. "As requested, one single room and one double."

"Thank you," the three friends said in unison.

"If you need me, I'll be right over there," Cielo said pointing to a small room on the right side, where there was no ocean view.

Lea had not noticed that there were rooms on both sides of the corridor. The rooms on the right, away from the ocean seemed to be much smaller and scattered apart; those were the rooms for the guides.

"Sonia, you and I are sharing a room. I figured you would be OK with that considering we shared one for so many years in college, and Kara is taking the single room," Lea said quickly organizing the sleeping arrangements.

"Great," Sonia said as she brought her bags into the room and placed them on one of the beds.

The rooms were full of light and sparsely furnished. A wool rug was placed between the beds and was the only rug in the room. The beds were small and covered with white cotton blankets.

A closet with sliding doors next to the entrance door was all there was for them to put away their belongings. There was a white tiled bathroom with one sink, shower, and toilet that connected them to Kara's room on the other side.

Wide-open windows brought the ocean into the room, pure and majestic. The soothing breaking of the waves and the salty air was fully present in their space.

Lea took a deep breath as she closed her eyes and sat on the opposite bed. She rearranged her pillow to be on the other end of the bed so that she could lie down and look out the window. She stretched herself on the bed and smiled.

"I'm not sure about you, Sonia, but I don't know how we got into this whole trip but this alone feels good. I'm willing to do whatever they tell me to do, just to be able to sleep with this view, this sound, and this air," Lea said relishing in the warmth, with the sun on her face. It was almost five o'clock by now and the sun was beginning its descent right in front of their window. "We will be able to see the sunset right from our beds."

"It's nice," Sonia said looking through the window

and then at her belongings. "What was I thinking when I packed all this?"

Lea could hear the sound of frustration in her friend's voice. "Let me help you," she said jumping up from her bed and helping her friend figure out what to take out and what to leave in her suitcase.

"Hello, ladies," said a deep voice from the door.

"Oh, hi Alex," Lea said looking up in surprise as she was helping Sonia lift her suitcase full of clothes for her stay in Miami on to the top shelf of their closet.

"Let me help you with that," Alex said quickly stepping into the room and easily grabbing the bag and placing it on the top shelf. Lea felt her voice a little shaky as she thanked him. There was something about this man that made her nervous, jittery.

"You are welcome. Are you coming to the first gathering? It's in ten minutes in the main lobby," he said to Lea as he left the room.

"We'll be over in a minute," Lea responded. She realized they needed to change. Sonia was still wearing her traveling outfit, and Lea needed to get into something cool, as her traveling clothes were now too warm for the Costa Rica heat.

They walked barefoot to the main lobby. It felt strange joining the other people as they walked down the corridor, all with bare feet. There were people of all ages, men and women. Lea noticed those she thought had been there before and were avid practitioners of yoga and its life-style and those that were rocky participants like her. The yogis had an air of serenity in their faces that she did not find in the others. A woman with long white hair came out of her room right in front of Lea as she walked down the hall. Lea did not see her face. She could see only her long lean body, her white hair falling on her shoulders. She was wearing loose linen pants and a flowing matching top that gave every step an ethereal air.

As the woman turned to acknowledge and welcome Lea, her deep blue eyes set on her and Lea felt as if she could see all the way into her very soul.

"Welcome to the center," the woman said to her, with the same hand gesture Lea was now starting to find most people made as they greeted each other. "My name is Ruth."

Lea and Sonia seated themselves on the yoga mats laid out for everyone in the main entrance, from where everyone could see the sea. Kara was already there, talking with people sitting around her.

"Welcome everyone to the Kalawi Yoga Center. I know many of you have been here before. Year after year you come back to reconnect with yourself and deepen your experience in your journey. For those who are here for the first time, welcome and we are blessed by your company," a woman, sitting high on a raised platform, said to the large crowd. Over seventy people were there, sitting on mats with their legs crossed in front of them, their hands, palms up, resting on their thighs.

"My name is Lama Alma," she said. She also sat with her legs crossed, her hands, palms up, resting on her thighs. Her back was straight and she was wearing loose flowing pants and a long top in shades of orange and mustard, colors that blended with the oranges and yellows of the setting sun behind her, placing her as suspended in the horizon.

The introductory comments were short and to the point. Every new guest was to be assigned to an experienced participant to guide them through the week, to act as a counselor, a guide.

Leaving the lobby, they were guided downstairs to an open area where low tables were set up all around the room, which was open to the beach. This served as the dining room.

Dark wooden floors and beautiful woodwork were everywhere, polished and varnished, giving the room an elegant and sophisticated look even though it was bare of any luxury.

Her counselor guided Lea to a low table in the back of the room while Sonia was being ushered to a table closer to the beach.

Soft, colorful cushions were placed around each square table, fitting two guests on each side for a total of eight guests per table. Bamboo placemats and small porcelain cups, or bowls, were neatly arranged for each setting.

"Here we go," Lea's guide said as she showed Lea her place at the table. "My name is Magdalena, and I'm honored to guide you this week," she said to Lea, as they had not been introduced to each other before sitting down at the table.

"My name is Lea," Lea tried to find a comfortable position on the cushion. She was very hungry, as they had had no food since they landed hours earlier and she was looking forward to a nice dinner. The sun had set now and the temperature had gone down to a comfortable seventies. From where Lea was seated, she could see glimpses of the bright white foam, as the waves kissed the shore in a rhythmical dance.

"Where are you from?" Lea asked as other guests began joining them at the table.

"I'm from Chile," Magdalena answered. "I've been coming here once a year for five years now," she said as she gestured with her hands a welcome to the other couples joining them.

Lea guessed Magdalena was about her own age, maybe a few years older but not by much. She had a serene peaceful look. Here dark black hair was pulled back in a low bun, her white skin was smooth and clear, while some light lines surrounded her eyes and mouth. Her dark eyes were clean, sharp, awake, framed by dark eyebrows that gave her an interesting, magical look of wisdom.

"I did not come last year, as my house was destroyed during the earthquake, and I lost everything, including my husband of thirty years," she said with clear voice. The serenity in her voice conveyed no self-pity. She told of her loss to allow the listener to connect with her.

Lea remembered hearing the news about the earthquake and had checked with Sonia and her family to make sure none of them were affected by it. Argentineans often traveled to Chile for business.

"I'm sorry," was all that Lea could say.

"Don't be— it's part of my journey," Magdalena said with a wide smile.

"Namaste," said Alex as he and his guest came over to the table. He was to be the guide of a man in his sixties.

"Good to see you, Alex," Magdalena said gesturing and bowing to Alex as he seated himself. Lea felt her face burning as he sat at the table opposite her.

Lea glanced around the table; the contrast between the guides and the first-time guests was impressive. The guests, independent of their age, looked old and tired. Their skin lacked shine, and their eyes were dull. *Is that how I look too?*

A young girl wearing a flowing linen dress approached their table, and kneeling graciously, placed two bowls in the center of the table. One of the bowls contained some kind of dark rice, maybe brown rice, Lea thought, and the other bamboo bowl contained what looked like a vegetable stir-fry of some sort.

Another girl, wearing the same kind of outfit as the first, poured tea in each of their small cups.

"Enjoy," the girls said as they moved on to the next table.

Before they touched the food, Alex took the lead and clasping his hands in front of him and closing his eyes, he said a few words in Hindi that Lea did not understand. He then grabbed a spoon and served each of the guests a serving of rice and a serving of vegetables. Before anybody else touched their forks, he grabbed his and sampled his food, closing his eyes as he savored it. Everybody watched him. Opening his eyes he smiled and gestured for everybody else to follow his example.

With this prompt, everyone around the table took a bite and closed their eyes savoring this first bite, including Lea.

Lea ate in silence while they all talked. , They introduced each other and shared their backgrounds. For someone who was always talkative and outgoing, Lea remained uncharacteristically silent throughout the dinner. She was enjoying every bite, savoring the meal, breathing between forkfuls, and taking time to nourish herself. She was embodying her experience; she was being present to her meal.

After a twenty-minute meditation after dinner, the group separated and made their way back to their rooms. Alex caught up to Lea who was ahead of him in the corridor. "You were very quiet over dinner. I hope you are doing OK," he said as he walked next to her.

"I was just enjoying dinner and enjoying everyone's conversation. I'm usually the one to talk first, but this time it felt good to just listen," she said wondering why she was giving so much information to this stranger.

"Well, if there's anything I can do to help you during

your stay, please let me know. The first time can be hard and awkward, but if you allow yourself to be immersed in the whole program, you will experience miracles," he said his voice deep and low next to her. The hallway to the rooms was lit only by candles placed along the wall in old lanterns hanging from iron hooks nailed to the wall.

Lea lay on her bed that night awake. Sonia had come in before her and had already been in bed, texting and checking email as Lea came in.

"Did you not give in your cell phone when we checked in?" Lea was surprised to see her friend texting and sending email.

"I know, I said I didn't have any," Sonia said admitting her lie. "But I promise I won't use it, I am just sending a message to Francisco to let him know we got here all right. I just don't want to be fully disconnected from my family."

"I sent Paul an email from the airport when we landed, and I left all the phone numbers in case he needs to reach me as Kara had told me that they would confiscate our phones," Lea said getting herself ready for bed.

There was no electricity in the rooms so she knew that Sonia's phone would not last long without being recharged.

There was not much to do once she got in bed as her pile of books laid untouched on the bureau. With just candlelight it was hard to read so she blew out her candle and lay on her bed.

There was something bothering her, and she could not figure out what. The place was beautiful, the scenery, the ocean, everything was breathtaking. She had enjoyed dinner and had not minded the meditation, but as she replayed in her mind the last few hours trying to find what was bothering her, she kept coming back to those instances since their arrival, that she had contact with Alex, the stranger that had helped them with their bags at the airport and who rode in the van with them. There was something about him that made her smile and nervous at the same time. He slightly brushed her arm against his as they walked back to their rooms that night, and she felt a bolt of electricity go through her body. It took her by surprise.

CHAPTER 10

Lea had woken up with the sun at 5:30 AM. She had finally fallen into a deep relaxed sleep and could barely remember where she was when she opened her eyes. Sonia slept next to her, a pillow on her head to avoid the light.

Breakfast had consisted of a green smoothie that was brought to them as the whole group sat in a giant circle in the main lobby.

"Drink this and allow your body to rebuild itself, clean and rejuvenate," said the leader as Sonia and Lea looked at each other suspiciously. Kara, seated right next to Lea, encouraged them to drink it and they could see everyone around them taking in the green foamy drink as sacred.

After that, and having previously done an hour of yoga in the upstairs room, Lea and Sonia walked down to the beach to take advantage of their free hour.

"That was disgusting," Sonia said as their feet touched the soft sand. They walked along the shore, lifting their loose pants as the waves came in toward them.

"It was, but it felt great. I actually feel more awake now than when we finished yoga," Lea had said recognizing the power of the drink.

They walked in silence for a few minutes when Lea suddenly stopped and said to Sonia. "Do you ever wonder where you are going with your life?" Sonia looked at her in surprise.

"What do you mean?" Sonia had said. "Not sure I follow you."

"Well, I'm thirty-nine years old, I'm well over the baby stage, my kids don't really want much from me these days, except for Lauren, and she is growing up fast too," Lea said gesturing with her hands, "and sometimes I wonder what I am supposed to do with my life."

"I have not worked in years, and I'm not sure what I would be good at these days anyway. I'm so out of everything. I don't really follow fashion much anymore, just the basics, and I have lost contacts with all my old colleagues and people in the magazine industry," she said referring to her past career, a career that died for Lea the moment she left New York and moved to Massachusetts. She had done some freelance writing for a while but soon after Colin was born that had ended as well.

"I feel like I'm stuck in this aging body but in my mind I have not even started living. I find that Paul and I don't share that much anymore other than the house and kids, I feel stuck and lost," Lea said her voice rising as she connected with herself and let go of her frustration and her anger.

"Well, have you talked to Paul about this?" Sonia asked trying to find a way to help her friend. Sonia could not relate to her friend—their lives were so different.

Sonia was a "*stay at home mother*," but the title did not compare to an average American mother. Sonia lived in Buenos Aires during the school year with her three children. Her boys were picked up every morning and taken to school, and they did not come home until five in the afternoon. A full-time maid and cook left time for Sonia to focus on decorating the place and socializing with her friends.

She belonged to a few charitable organizations that put up major social events during the fall and winter season. There was the gala at the Teatro Colon and the Hospital Dinner at one of the French palaces now used mostly for weddings and social events.

For each of these events, Sonia had a personal seamstress that custom made her gowns, ensuring that she always wore one of a kind pieces.

A few times a year, Sonia traveled with her husband, a successful polo player turned investor. They went to Paris, did safaris in Africa, cruises through the Panama Canal, Italy, and Hong Kong. Sonia's mother moved into her house on those occasions and ruled over the house, which was easy when the house was fully staffed, including a live-in tutor who takes over the children full time when Sonia and her husband travel.

Sonia's life had a purpose and she loved it. She had been able to keep the relationship with her husband alive, and she saw her children enough to enjoy them but not too much that they interfered with her life.

"Maybe you and Paul just need a vacation," Sonia said with a smile completely at a loss for words or ideas how to support her friend.

"That's not the point, I feel hollow in here," Lea said touching her chest. "I am lost within my soul. I don't recognize who I am anymore, nor what I want, nor where I want to be in ten years," Lea said as they resumed their walk. Lea's voice transparent with emotion as she for the first time allowed herself to open up and put words to her emotions.

"Well, then maybe this might be a good trip for you, Maybe this trip will help you reconnect with yourself and figure it out," Sonia said as they saw other people walking along the beach.

"Do you remember back in college, when I said I wanted to be a famous novelist and write all these books about people and how they cope with difficulties? Remember?" Lea said referring to their past life, those years when they shared a room and shared their dreams.

"Yes, I do," Sonia said. "What happened to that dream? Are you still writing?"

"I got married and I stopped focusing on my dreams." Lea said regretfully.

"But Lea you have a beautiful family, you love being with your kids, I know you do," Sonia said trying to bring her friend back to her life, back to what she knew her friend loved in spite of her words. "You also talked about how you wanted to be a mother, how you wanted a house full of kids, a house full of life."

"I know you are right, I did dream all of that, so why do I feel like I'm lost, like I don't know where I left myself or how to find myself?" Lea asked now talking more to herself than to her friend.

"I was talking to a friend of mine, she turned forty-two this year, and she was telling me how she had gone through this mini-crisis as she was turning forty. She began wondering what she had done with her life, where she was going, just like you," Sonia said remembering a conversation she had had with this friend a few months ago. "It's possible that this is all part of where you are. It's a phase that we must go through as we reach the famous forties," she said though she did not feel that way herself.

"Maybe you are right," Lea said as they turned around and began their walk back to the center. Lea felt the emotion, she allowed herself to feel and her voice had a trace of frustration, as she knew her friend was not really getting what she was experiencing.

"Did you hear that tomorrow is a silent day? We are not allowed to talk all day, not even if we need a glass of water or anything," Lea said as she reminded her friend of the coming schedule.

"That sucks," Sonia said. Lea wondered how much her friend was enjoying the experience. She knew this was not Sonia's typical trip.

"Are you doing OK with the trip?" Lea asked as they reached the front of the center.

"It's OK. I think by the time we are done, I will have enjoyed it. It's just more work than I'm used to doing," Sonia said honestly.

"I know but I think it's just what I need. You might be right, this might be just a phase because I am turning forty soon, and maybe Kara was right in bringing me here. I'm just so happy you could come with me too," Lea said squeezing Sonia's hand as they climbed up the steps back to the center.

Lea woke up to a bell chime ringing down the hall, soft and hollow. As she opened her eyes she reconnected with where she was. The sun again reflected on the waves breaking right under her window.

As she left her room she ran into other guests that greeted her with a smile, a bow, clasping their palms in front of their chests reminding her it was "silent" day.

She wondered what it would be like to spend a day without uttering a word, on top of being completely isolated technologically, no phone, no email, no texting, nothing.

She placed her yoga mat at the far corner overlooking the beach. She had been late the day before so she had to take a spot in the back of the room, but today thanks to the bell she managed to find for herself a great spot for the morning yoga.

Slowly the room filled up with the other guests, all-smiling but not talking to each other. The first rays of sun were starting to light the room; Lea guessed it was around 6 AM, but it was hard to tell without a watch. She sat on her toes as she focused her eyes on the horizon.

Feeling a stir next to her she found Alex placing his mat right next to hers, only four or five inches separating her purple sticky mat from his green sticky mat.

He smiled at her and bowed as he unrolled his towel and placed it on the floor next to his mat. He took a seat on his matt, his legs crossed, his hands, palms up, resting on his knees, his eyes on the horizon.

Lea could feel his presence. She could hear his breathing, she could sense the warmth of his body even though they were a few feet from each other, and she could even smell him, a smell of sweat and vanilla, a smell of warmth and virility.

She closed her eyes and took a deep breath, her mind fully aware of the moment, miles away from her home, her husband, her reality. She allowed herself to feel what she felt at the moment, a magnetic attraction to a man she hardly knew, a stranger.

They went through the motions, led by the Lama, in complete silence. The sound of their breath, the sound of their movements on the mat as they lifted their feet, moved on through the poses, arrived into each pose breathing deeply, inhaling and exhaling through the nose with a soft hollow rhythm.

It was a deep soothing experience, her body moving in synch with Alex and the rest of the guests. Lea felt alive, empowered like she had never felt before; an energy that moved from her toes to the top of her head filling her with light, awakening her senses.

As they finished the meditation, after their practice, Lea opened her eyes and again stared at the distance.

They were again handed a green smoothie as soon as they finished the yoga session. Lea's muscles were starting to act up after so many downward facing dogs in just a couple of days, but she felt like her body was responding well. She felt cleaned and relaxed, her body detoxing and slimming.

They were led out of the yoga room and back into the lobby where a chanting session was taking place. Lea caught up with Sonia as they followed the crowd and took seats on the mats arranged on the veranda, outside.

Crossing their legs and placing their hands on their

knees, palms up, they followed the leader in deep Ommm's. Sonia smiled and looked at Lea as she tried to imitate the sound but seeing that Lea was fully concentrated in her practice Sonia gave up and focused on hers.

Lea felt her chest opening and her heart lifting as she allowed to be led in deep chanting that rose from her groin, through her stomach, up her chest, through her neck and out her mouth, echoing along the way and making her whole torso and head tremble with the hollow sounds from within her.

As she mastered the experience, she relaxed into it, allowing her voice to grow stronger and stronger with every inhale, her body vibrating with every chant, and exhale. It was sensual and invigorating.

As their afternoon meditating session came to an end, Lea ran into Alex as they left the room.

Gesturing with his hands Lea followed Alex outside where he led her out onto the beach.

She wasn't sure where they were going or what she was doing, but she wanted to follow him. They walked in silence along the beach, the sun setting, light illuminating their shadows as they walked. Lea looked up to him, he smiled at her leading her farther away from the center.

As they reached the cliffs at the end of the long

stretch of beach, he walked away from the shore to a flat spot where he took a seat, cross-legged, his hands on his knees, palms up.

Lea followed his example and sat next to him, on the warm sand, far away from him so as not to touch but close enough to feel him next to her.

Closing his eyes, he began breathing rhythmically; deep inhales followed by deep exhalations every time. Lea followed his example.

Within seconds they were breathing in synch, the ocean breeze on their face, the salty scent in their nose. There was a physical connection between them that overwhelmed Lea, as her body's breathing pattern was taken over by this stranger. Lea allowed herself to relax into it, to be present in it.

Within a few breaths Alex began moving through yoga poses with Lea following his lead. Now they were not just breathing in synch, they were also moving in synch. Their arms pushing their bodies from downward facing dog down to a plank and into snake, their chest opening as they bent their elbows with every move, their chins lifting, their faces up to the last rays of sun as they began a new vinyasa.

It was exhilarating and relaxing.

They moved in this way for a few repetitions until finally settling back down into their seated pose, this time facing each other, the sunlight filtering between them landed on the sand, creating deep shadows in the uneven surface. The white sand now reflected shades of purple, pink, and red.

Opening his eyes, Alex lifted up a hand, palm-facing Lea and encouraged her to do the same. Lea suspended her right hand, palm facing Alex, in front of his left hand.

Their palms were not touching, but Lea could feel his warmth, his energy, traveling through her hand down her arm and into her body. A warm feeling surrounded her and as she closed her eyes into it she felt his palm, straight and engaged coming to rest on her palm.

She felt a shock and opened her eyes as he smiled and closed his eyes again into the feeling. Lifting his right hand he encouraged her to do the same.

With both palms connected Lea melted in the warmth of his energy. Not a word was said. They remained this way until the sun set beyond the horizon, until the deep shadows on the sand became deep dark gray and black valleys around them, until the ocean air changed into a cool breeze.

As they brought their hands down and opened their eyes they both smiled, a wide honest deep smile of connection like Lea had never experienced before.

Alex stood up and Lea followed. They walked back to the center. Their bodies again moved in synch, without a word being exchanged.

As Lea returned to her room that evening Sonia was already there, getting ready for bed. Recognizing her friend's focused state of relaxation, Sonia did not push Lea to break her silence, even though she was dying to talk, for she had seen Lea walk away from the center with Alex at sunset.

Lea lay in her bed wondering what it was that she had experienced that day. It was not just that moment with Alex on the beach, it was their synchronized yoga session, and it was the whole day in silence. She experienced a level of physical and mental content she had never experienced before. She was not thinking about her life back in Massachusetts; she was relishing in that moment.

CHAPTER 11

Lea could not make sense of what she had experienced with Alex the previous day. As she walked out of her room and into their morning yoga, she looked for him in the yoga room before placing her mat and was disappointed to not find him. She placed her mat next to Kara instead who was already seated, cross-legged with her eyes closed. Sonia came and sat next to them as well.

Another green smoothie followed their practice and while there was no "silence rule" that day, people were either keeping silent or talking in very low whispers.

Alex met her in the lobby and again gestured her to follow him. She walked down the steps to the beach right behind him. She was puzzled by what she felt, her reaction to him, and her physical need of his presence.

"How are you feeling?" he asked in his accented English as they walked down the beach. The sun was high up and it was warm.

"Good, what was that last evening? I've never experienced anything like that," Lea said opening up right away. She knew they did not have much time together considering that the week at the center was almost over and she had a need to understand what it was that she was experiencing.

"A physical and spiritual connection," he said lightly as if it happened to him every day.

"Oh," Lea said wondering.

"It's a very special thing that does not happen often. I felt your energy and your need to connect from the moment we met in the van," he said explaining further.

"I felt you were lost and you needed to come back to your soul, to embrace yourself and go back to your essence," Alex said as he looked at her as they walked.

"I felt a connection with you that is rare and special,"

he continued, making Lea feel special and reciprocated in her feelings.

"But, Lea, this is something special we shared yesterday, something unique and rare," he continued scaring Lea with his words.

"Alex, I'm a married woman," Lea said now connecting with her reality and feeling somehow ashamed for allowing herself that moment with him.

"I know," Alex said. "What happened between us is a combination of spirits and timing. We found each other in a time and place where we could give each other what we needed at that moment," Alex said somehow trying to release Lea from her guilt and her feelings of betrayal.

"It was perfect," Lea said in a whisper.

"You are perfect," Alex said standing in front of her and bringing his palm up for her to connect with him.

"Thank you," Lea said in a whisper, raising her palm and closing her eyes, allowing a tear to roll down her cheek. It had been a long time since she had felt this deep connection with anyone, a long time since she had felt perfect and wonderful and full of life.

"While we connected with each other and you gave me what I needed and I gave you what you needed, we were only acting as mirrors for each other. What we reached is a deep connection with ourselves," Alex said as their palms felt each other's warmth. "What we allowed each other is to connect with ourselves and thus allowed us to connect with each other."

Lea listened, her eyes closed, the sun shining strong above them. She could feel sweat building on her brow and above her lip. It was not the sunset light and soft breeze from the previous evening.

As they walked back to the center for lunch, Lea replayed Alex's words in her head. She could still feel his positive energy and his peaceful expression next to her, but she was also beginning to feel some of that energy and peace herself.

"What was all that about?" Sonia asked as she caught up with Lea on the way to lunch in the outdoor patio.

"What?" Lea asked acting surprised.

"What's all that walking on the beach with the guy from the van?" Sonia said annoyed by her friend asking her to be that explicit.

"Nothing," Lea said in her new calm, relaxed voice.

"He is an amazing human being and he has been helping me connect with myself," Lea said trying to keep the conversation to the minimum, not inclined to explain much to her friend.

"I find that I'm relaxed and energized. I find myself

connecting with myself and finding peace within me," Lea said trying to sum up what was going through her at the moment.

"I am kind of relaxed," Sonia said. "Maybe even in spite of myself," she said almost thinking out loud.

Lea was trying to make sense of her feelings again that afternoon wondering how she could go back to her real life after this spiritual experience. She knew she cherished her life and her family—she even found herself missing her children. And after the experience with Alex she missed her husband and wanted to connect deeply with him.

True, she had fantasized of a romantic experience with this stranger, but deep inside her respect and loyalty for her husband were stronger and she began to miss him physically and emotionally.

As they finished their dinner and walked out of their last meditation of the day, Lea caught up with Kara as she was walking to her room.

"So how do you go to real life from here?" Lea asked hoping for some answers from her yoga friend.

"I saw you walking with Alex," Kara said. "I've met him before in other retreats. He is a well-known spiritual guide and experienced healer," she continued. "You are very lucky to have spent time with him," Kara said.

"Yes, I know," Lea said wondering if his reaching out to her was because he sensed her need or because he was attracted to her.

"It can be hard to go from this to everyday life but that is the challenge. It gets easier with time and the more you practice the harvesting of your inner self, the easier it is to transition from a full-time practice like we've been doing here to a balanced life," Kara said as they stopped in front of Lea's door.

"I worry that I will go into culture shock when we go home in two days," Lea said feeling the pressure of her anxiety in her chest.

"Don't focus on that yet. The exercises we do in the next few days will help you, very gently, find answers to your question, but you are still in the middle of it," Kara said as they finished their conversation and Lea went into her room.

Sonia was sitting on her bed, her eyes red from crying.

"What happened?" Lea said as she ran to her friend and sat next to her.

"Nothing. It's this magical environment," Sonia said rubbing her nose and quickly trying to hide her tears.

"No, it's not, what's going on?" Lea asked hugging her now and wondering what could have happened in the last half hour to bring her friend to this state. She was holding her phone on her lap.

"Francisco is having an affair," Sonia burst out looking at Lea.

"He is what?" Lea said not believing her words. "You guys were just in Uruguay on a romantic getaway. And the two of you go out on dates and mini honeymoons all the time. I don't think I know any other couple that spends more time together than the two of you," Lea said trying to figure out what her friend was saying.

"I've suspected for the last six months, but he has changed lately. He has been so attentive, so caring. We had a great time in Uruguay that weekend, getting the house ready for the summer. He bought me a beautiful ring for my birthday and arranged a surprise dinner party with all our friends at my favorite restaurant.

"But he has also taken more weekend "work" trips lately, and he has not been home for dinner more often. The kids have hardly seen him lately," she continued between sobs. "I texted my mum, just now, asking if Francisco had been around much this past weekend. He told me he would stay home and spend time with the kids. Well, apparently he did not come home Saturday night, and he showed up Sunday morning with croissants for everyone as if he had woken up early and gone out. My mum checked his room; he had not slept there," Sonia said her hands shaking, using her sleeve as a handkerchief.

"But you still don't know for sure," Lea said, not even convincing herself with that statement.

"I know, I really have known for a while. I just didn't want to admit it. I was pretending we were fine, pretending I was wrong, but I've known it all along. And now, I will have to face him when I go home. I can't do that. I love my life, I love our relationship. I love him and the kids. This is what I've always wanted," Sonia said sobbing between thoughts, her tears now pouring out.

Lea hugged her friend, but she had no words for her. She had envied her friend's marriage, her life, her luxuries, and now she realized that no one could see it all from the outside. She realized how wrong she had been to assume that her friend had the perfect life.

CHAPTER 12

Lea was not ready for the end of their stay. Many of the guests had left earlier that morning. Lea and her friends were now waiting for the van to drive them to the airport.

"Good-bye, Lea," Alex said as he came to her in the lobby.

"Good-bye," Lea said looking up into his eyes, trying to find a shared sparkle, a shared sadness, but she only found peace. She found clarity and brightness.

"Don't be sad. I can feel your emptiness," Alex said as he guided Lea away from her friends so that they could talk in private. The van was not there yet, and they had some time.

"I feel drained," Lea said, thick tears in the corner of her eyes. "I feel sad, with a sadness I had not experienced before and I'm scared," she said as she looked up to her new friend.

The week had been intense for Lea and learning about Sonia's marriage troubles had made Lea really connect with that part of her own life. Her feelings for Alex scared her, but she felt a strong sense of belonging and loyalty to Paul and her children. She knew that she and Paul had a relationship of trust. Seeing Sonia's suffering, she knew she would never put her husband in that situation. But her feelings for Alex were strong, maybe stronger than anything she had experienced before.

"Our journey is ours to walk. You will find partners and guides along the way, but don't forget that what you hold true is yourself. You have to live honest to your beliefs and to your needs. I find you incredibly attractive and I'm spiritually drawn to you," he said making Lea blush. "But we are not meant to journey together right now other than the days we shared here. Maybe, who knows, the future might bring us back together, but for now you have a family to go back to," he said with a shy smile exposing his feelings for her in a way that Lea could hardly understand but could sense as true.

As the van arrived, Lea and her two traveling companions placed their bags in the trunk and climbed into the van. Lea looked out the window, deep sadness surrounding her as she shyly waved to Alex who was standing at the curb waving good-bye.

Sonia, seated in the middle seat between Lea and Kara, kept her eyes down clutching her purse. She had shrunk in the last two days, wearing no makeup, her buoyance gone from her. Lea held her hand as the van drove away.

"You'll be fine," Lea whispered to Sonia as they headed to the airport. Kara and Lea shared a sad compassionate smile over Sonia's head as Kara kept to herself, respecting Sonia's grief.

"I don't know how I am going to face him, my children, my life," Sonia started again between sobs as her body shook under Lea's embrace.

"I want to disappear, I can't go back home, I want to disappear," she repeated in whispers as her clenched hand rubbed a handkerchief over her face.

Sonia had canceled her stay in Miami and had decided to fly straight home. She did not have the energy to go partying in Miami after all. Her mother was picking her up at the airport and they had decided that Sonia and her children and would stay over at her mother's weekend house the first weekend home. For now she had not given her husband any indication of what she knew, and she wanted to be in Buenos Aires for a couple of days before confronting him.

As they hugged each other after the security clearance at the airport, Lea reassured Sonia that it would all be all right. There was no right answer, no one-way to solve this problem.

"I want to kill him, that's what I want," Sonia said with clenched teeth.

"Talk to him, he is a good person. You two have shared a long and wonderful relationship, maybe he is struggling with something, maybe he is having his own crisis, or maybe you are wrong. Talk to him and be straightforward before you jump to conclusions," Lea said still not sure how this wonderfully loving partner could be cheating on his long-time beautiful wife.

"You are right," Sonia said as she rubbed her eyes and adjusted her purse. Her stilettoes and big hair had been put away. She was beautiful with her clean face, ponytailed blond hair, simple jeans, and white shirt.

"Have a good flight and call me as soon as you can, I'll be expecting your call," Lea said as they walked in opposite directions.

Kara and Lea found their seats on the plane, stashed their carry-on bags in the overhead compartment, sat and fastened their seatbelts. Lea was now sitting in the middle seat while Kara sat next to the window.

"So, what do you think? Was this what you expected?" Kara asked as people kept coming into the plane and taking their seats.

"More than I expected," Lea said peacefully. "Had I known that we would be doing yoga two times a day, having green smoothies for breakfast, meditation, no electricity, no sugar, no coffee, no wine… I would probably not have come. But it was exactly what I needed," she said recognizing her friend's wisdom. "So thank you for bringing me and for not telling me much about it beforehand," she said as she placed her hands on her flat stomach feeling good about herself.

She had not stepped on a scale but she could feel that she had lost at least five to ten pounds in one week of eating healthy foods and moving her body.

"I feel great. I feel lighter, at peace, and while sad to leave, I look forward to being with my family," she said to her friend as the plane began taxiing down the runway.

"I'm glad. It was good for me as well. I needed to reconnect and slow down," Kara said as she closed her eyes and clenched her hands over the armrest. Lea could feel her friend's soft deep breathing as the plane ascended to its cruising altitude.

Boston Logan Airport welcomed them with a light snow covering the runway. It was late afternoon and pitch dark.

"It's only five o'clock and it's night time here," Kara exclaimed as they taxied to the gate, her forehead relaxing.

"I'm not ready for cold again," Lea said closing her eyes and leaning her head against her seat.

It was seven o'clock by the time they made it back home. Lea dropped Kara off at her house before continuing on to hers.

"Call me in the morning," Kara said hugging her friend. "And remember, be kind to yourself and to your family. They have no idea where you've been, so don't expect them to understand and match your peaceful stress-free mood right now."

"I know," Lea said preparing herself to face her routine and her responsibilities.

As she opened the side door and pushed her bags in, Lea smelled the wood burning in the fireplace. Missy came running to her as she heard the door open, and behind her came Lauren and Paul.

"Welcome home, Mummy. I missed you!" said Lauren giving her a big hug around her hips as Lea put down her purse and coat.

"Welcome home, honey," Paul said reaching over Lauren and gently kissing his wife on the lips.

"Thank you," Lea said smiling and kneeling down to hug Lauren at her height. She took a second longer than usual to hug her daughter. She smelled her hair and allowed herself to feel and receive the hug.

"We missed you," her husband said as he took her into his arms and held her tight. Lauren ran off with Missy excited to show her mother what she and her siblings had been working on.

"I missed you too," Lea said, a sense of guilt on her heart as she said what her husband needed to hear but not necessarily the truth. Nevertheless she focused on his embrace. Focused on feeling, receiving his hug as well as hugging him. She reminded herself of her friend Sonia and her heartbreaking journey home. She thought of Alex and his wisdom; and she reminded herself also that she and Paul were journeying together and that they had chosen to do so years ago and that commitment was still strong between them.

"So what's the big surprise?" Lea asked as Paul took her hand and led her to the kitchen.

"I can't tell," he said mysteriously.

"Hi Mum," Jenny said coming out of the kitchen. "Hi Jenny," Lea said wishing she could hug her teenage daughter but respecting her distance.

"Hey Mum, how was your trip?" Colin said as he came out of the playroom, TV control in hand. "You should have seen this house while you were gone; it was a disaster," he said as he brushed his arms around his mother quickly in a halfhearted embrace.

"Mommy, Mommy, let me put this on you," Lauren said as she came up to Lea and urged her to lean down so she could tie a bandana around her eyes.

"What?" Lea said looking up to her husband with a questioning smile.

Lauren and the other children led Lea to the living room.

"Surprise!" the three of them screamed as Paul untied the bandana.

The lights were dim and they had put the coffee table in front of the fireplace with a tablecloth, flowers, plates, and silverware. A big bowl of pasta was placed in the middle with sauce and salad.

A strong fire was humming softly in the fireplace, and Lea welcomed the soothing warm atmosphere her family had created for her.

"This is beautiful, thank you," Lea, said relishing in her loved ones' gesture to make her feel welcomed and missed.

Jenny had arranged pillows around the coffee table;

many had come from the beds upstairs.

Lea smiled as they seated themselves on the floor, welcoming the familiarity of what she had done for the past week at the center.

"Did you know that this is how we ate every day at the Yoga Center?" Lea said as she placed her napkin on her lap.

"There are no tables and chairs there. They all sit on the floor, on pillows, around low tables," she explained as she sat back allowing her husband to serve the food and pass it around. She gestured to him to serve her very little pasta and she filled her plate with the spinach and carrot salad they had prepared for their meal.

"Really?" Lauren asked surprised. "They don't have real tables and chairs?" she asked as she picked up her fork. "Can we do this every night?"

"Well, why don't we try something else new? Let's all pray together before we eat," Lea said offering her hand to her daughter Jenny seating next to her.

"Hmm, OK," Paul said not sure how to react.

"I am thankful for being home with my family," Lea said leading the prayer.

"I am thankful for Mummy being back home with us," Paul said following his wife's example.

"I'm thankful because it's Friday and I can watch TV until late," Colin said with a smirk.

"I'm thankful for the sleepover I'm having tomorrow at Sophie's house," Jenny said with her teenage voice making fun of the exercise with her tone but still participating. Lea rolled her eyes and smiled to her husband.

"And I'm thankful for the ice cream Daddy bought for dessert!" Lauren said with a wide smile.

They ate leisurely while talking about their week and bringing Lea up to date with the latest events.

By the time dinner was cleared and the kitchen was cleaned up it was nine o'clock and Lea put Lauren to bed as she had already watched a couple of movies that afternoon. Colin and Jenny were allowed to stay up for another movie that they would watch in the playroom in the basement.

"I missed you, Mummy," Lauren said as she put her arms around her mother. Lea was kneeling next to her bed, in the darkness, rubbing her back and singing a song.

"I missed you too, baby," Lea said laying her head next to her daughter's and kissing her cheek. "Sleep well. Tomorrow we can go for a walk on the beach," she said as she slowly walked out of the room.

"Ready?" Paul said as he met Lea in the corridor. He grabbed her hand and led her to their bedroom. The bed was nicely made and there was a small bouquet of flowers on her bedside table. A gift box had been placed on Lea's pillow.

"What is this?" Lea asked as she sat on her bed and grabbed the box.

Lea pulled on the ribbon and opened the box. A silk cream-colored negligée was carefully folded inside with a handwritten note from her husband that said "I missed you."

Lea leaned on the bed and kissed her husband who was sitting on the opposite side.

She was grateful for his efforts, for trying to reset their clock and using this opportunity to rekindle their love.

"I love you," she said as he pulled her to him and kissed her deeply. She meant it.

"Let me close the door," Paul said as Lea hopped off the bed and dimmed the lights.

She grabbed her gift and went to the bathroom. Lea felt her lightness as she changed into the negligée. She felt good in her body tonight, and she was ready to connect with her husband.

She walked toward him in the dim bedroom and Paul

placed his big hands on her hips, feeling the softness of the silk on her body.

"It feels good," he said closing his eyes and lowering his head to her shoulder. "You look amazing," he said kissing behind her ears as they slowly moved toward their bed. Lea relaxed into his touch.

CHAPTER 13

Lea kissed her daughter good-bye as she ran out the door to get the bus. It was Monday morning and after a whole weekend with her family, readjusting to her daily life, Lea now had a long day ahead of her.

While she finished loading the dishwasher and cleaned the kitchen, she thought about the good times they had shared as a family this past weekend.

They had gone for walks on the beach, the five of them. Jenny, Lauren, and Lea had spent some time in the kitchen on Sunday baking for the upcoming holidays while Paul and Colin worked on raking the leaves in the yard. It had been a homecoming for Lea in the true sense of the word. She had felt that as a family they were able to connect and cherish their time together.

As she hopped in the shower, Lea thought what was next for her. The week away had showed her how she needed to focus on her needs and dreams as much as her family's. What was she searching for herself? What was it that she wanted to engage her time and energy on?

Wearing a cozy warm turtleneck and loose black pants, she sat in front of her computer with a cup of tea and began looking at job listings in the area, her wet hair tied up in a ponytail. She did not want a full-time job, as it would be a challenge to manage the kids' schedule and the house, if she was gone all day and paying for a nanny would be too expensive.

She needed an identity beyond her children and her family life.

After an hour of staring at the computer screen wondering what direction she should go, Lea felt frustrated and decided to get some fresh air before the kids got home. Putting on her winter boots and jacket she walked out, her hands in her pockets, her mind in a whirlwind of thoughts. It was a beautiful late November day, and Lea felt the sun warming up her face as she walked aimlessly around her neighborhood.

Her home was surrounded by single-family homes with large backyards. Most of the homes had well cared landscaping that bloomed with multiple colors in the spring. Now, close to Thanksgiving weekend, the trees were bare and the dried-out lawns were still covered with the last remains of leaves that had yet to get picked up.

As Lea walked back to her house, her neighbor from down the street waved at her. She had gone out to get the mail when she saw Lea walking toward her. While they only lived a few houses apart, Lea rarely saw her neighbor Samantha out and about.

Lea stopped and they chitchatted standing next to the mailbox. Lea had an hour before the children came home from school and urged by her lonely neighbor she decided to accept her invitation to come in for a visit.

As they walked into the house, Samantha took her seat in the high stool by the kitchen counter where she had been sitting before getting the mail. It looked like she had not gone out much that day; she was wearing black lounge cashmere pants and a loose sweater. Her cigarette and ashtray sat in the middle of the kitchen counter. She offered Lea a glass of water, a cup of tea, or a glass of wine, even though it was only two in the afternoon. Lea smiled and said water would be perfect; she couldn't imagine sipping wine at that hour.

"Well, honey, it's so stressful with the house—there's always so much to do. I was thinking of hosting Thanksgiving for my family this year, but I am so tired these days," Samantha said as they continued the conversation they had started outside while she gave Lea a glass of water and poured a glass of wine for herself, alternating between a sip of wine and a puff of her cigarette while she talked. Her heavyset body overflowing the countertop stool where she sat.

Lea knew Samantha well enough to just let her talk. She knew that she craved company and an ear to hear her out. She was fine with doing that for a little bit, but the cigarette smoke was already beginning to bother her.

"Well, it's not that bad for me. The kids are getting older and they help around the house, and I feel like I need something outside of the house that I might enjoy that would challenge me intellectually," Lea said as she sipped from her glass of water, not sure why she was opening up her heart to her.

Samantha was in her mid-sixties and Lea had known her since they moved to the area. She had not changed much in the last fifteen years though. When Lea met her, her husband Rick was still alive and she had her stepchildren living with her part time. Lea remembered the children would watch TV most of the time while their father was at work, rarely playing outside or going out for walks. Samantha was too tired or too stressed to take care of them and take them to the beach in the summer or chauffeur them to and from their sports events.

Every now and then Samantha would embark on a new project, whether it was redecorating her house, fixing the kitchen, or taking a new online class. She mainly kept herself busy in the house.

Since the grocery store had begun doing home deliveries, Lea had noticed that Samantha would get a weekly delivery truck with the groceries so she suspected that she was not leaving the house, not even for food shopping these days.

Lea remembered how when she first moved to the area, after living most of her life in New York City, Samantha was one of the first people she met as she walked around the neighborhood with Paul one Saturday afternoon. They had met her by the mailbox as she was getting her mail. Lea had enjoyed the conversation with her that day, but as she had gotten to know her a little better she could not imagine a lonelier life than her neighbor's. Paul and Lea had once been invited for drinks when Samantha's husband was still alive, and they had sat, one summer evening, in the enclosed porch overlooking the backyard sipping root beer floats, something Lea had never tried before, while talking about the weather. Samantha had dressed up for the occasion, long red nails, a long bright-colored caftan, fake eyelashes, and heavy makeup. Lea had felt underdressed in her simple summer dress and sandals.

"So, are you heading to Florida this winter? I know how you don't like spending winters here, with the cold and everything," Lea asked just making conversation as she looked up at the clock on the wall making sure she still had time before the kids got home.

"Well, I don't know. Nowadays with all the security in the airports, traveling is not that much fun. I refuse to be fully scanned with those new machines, I think they violate privacy, and I've read that they can cause cancer," she said as she refilled her glass of wine.

"But you haven't been to your house on the beach for a long time now, have you?" Lea asked. Samantha and her late husband had bought a beautiful house on the beach a few years ago, and she remembered how Rick used to love talking about their beach house.

"I know. It's been busy around here and I really don't enjoy flying," Samantha said puffing out smoke and letting out a sigh.

"Well, thank you for the quick visit. I've got to go," Lea said as she hopped off the stool and headed out.

"The kids will be home any minute now," she said as she waved good-bye and let herself out.

She walked briskly back home, welcoming the brisk cold air on her face. She had only spent about ten minutes at Samantha's house, but it was long enough to smell of cigarette smoke.

Samantha had married Rick when she was very young, maybe in her mid-twenties. Rick had been divorced with two children and had met Samantha when she worked as a secretary in a local company. While her stepchildren had spent quite a bit of time at Samantha's growing up, Lea suspected that they had barely stayed in touch with her since their father died two years earlier. She knew the kids had moved away for college and had not had much reason to come back to the area. Their own mother had passed away a few years before as well.

As far as Lea knew, the two kids were now married, one living in London with his wife and kids and the other lived in New York with his partner.

Lea remembered having a long conversation with Rick, after a few drinks one winter night. Lea and Paul were having dinner at their house, on one of those rare occasions when Samantha had decided to put together dinner for a small group.

"I regret how it all ended up," Rick had whispered to

Lea as they sat long after the table had been cleared. Rick was a nice guy, gentle and easy to talk to, but he rarely expressed his feelings.

"I miss my children, I really do. I still remember when little Luke broke his arm, how I took him to the hospital and then I spent the night holding him as he was in so much pain. He was only three years old," Rick had said remembering his fathering years with his now forty-year-old estranged son.

"You should call them, reach out to them," Lea had said at the time, insisting that it was never too late to seek his children's forgiveness.

"It's too late, I've screwed up big," he had said in a whisper looking at his wife in the next room. Samantha was sitting in the living room, an empty bottle of wine next to her, loudly making her point to the crowd. She was rude and loud, and her guests just smiled politely as they let her talk, not daring to interrupt.

"It's never too late," Lea had said putting her hand on top of his.

It had been a rare and unexpected conversation. Lea recalled that soon after, Rick had been diagnosed with cancer and she had seen his kids come back and visit him during the yearlong battle with the illness. They had been with him when he died.

Rick had worked in his law firm until a week before he died. Lea thought that staying home full time with his wife must have been too dreadful to bear and he did not dare abandon his daily routine of going to the office. The successful law firm that he had built was taken over by his partner.

Lea had seen his children at the funeral. She thought it was the last time they had visited.

CHAPTER 14

"How are you doing?" Lea said as her friend Sonia picked up the phone. It was eleven in the morning in Massachusetts and one in the afternoon in Buenos Aires.

"Oh, hi Lea. How are you?" Sonia said recognizing her friend.

"I'm well. So how was your return, everything OK?" Lea asked too curious for chitchat.

The yoga retreat was more than a week ago now, and Lea had not heard anything from her friend since they hugged and said good-bye at the Costa Rica airport.

"Yes everything OK," Sonia said cryptically. "Let me call you in two minutes."

"What was that all about?" Lea asked as her phone rang.

"Francisco was standing right next to me," Sonia said as Lea could hear noise in the background.

"Where are you now?" Lea asked.

"I'm in my car, heading to the mall. I was just leaving the house when you called anyway, so I figure it was safer to talk from my cell," Sonia said.

"Things are going OK. When I landed in Buenos Aires, my mum picked me up and she already had the kids, so we spent the weekend at her house in Pilar. I knew Francisco was away that weekend; he had a polo tournament in Brazil so it was OK. He didn't even know I came back as I had changed my ticket when I canceled my stay in Miami, remember?" Sonia said as Lea could hear the loud horns in the background of Buenos Aires traffic.

She still remembered her visit to Buenos Aires for Sonia's engagement party. She and Paul had been in shock to see how people drove in the city. Nobody respected traffic lanes or stop signs. The stop signs were there, but nobody ever stopped at one. People crossed the street wherever they felt like, not at pedestrian crossings.

"We can talk later if you want to focus on your driving," Lea said worried about her friend swinging in and out of traffic while they talked.

"No, it's fine," Sonia said.

"So, when I came back, and after the weekend at Mum's, I was able to figure out a plan. I had decided that I would not let anger take the best of me. I would overcome my own reaction to figure out what was going on," Sonia said recounting the first few days back.

"Well, that's good. Anger will not solve anything, anyway," Lea said as she cradled the phone between her ear and her shoulder while she prepared herself a salad for lunch.

"I know. So the thing is, I asked Francisco to meet me for lunch a few days ago. I was shaking I was so nervous and he could see that," Sonia continued as Lea sat down with her plate full of greens in front of her.

"What's wrong, baby?" Francisco had asked Sonia as they met up for lunch. Sonia had mastered all her energy not to burst out crying and had carefully explained to her husband how she was certain that he was cheating on her.

"So what did he say?" Lea asked holding her breath.

"At first he denied it completely. He said it was my imagination, that he would never do that to me, and why was I thinking that way," Sonia said. "But I explained to him why I knew for certain that he was lying to me. I never once raised my voice. I could not believe myself. I wanted to meet him in a public place so that I would have a better chance of controlling myself," Sonia continued.

"He acknowledged his affair, he cried, he pleaded with me, I cried…"

Lea could hear her friend crying on the phone.

"The thing is, I love him. I can't find it in me to hate him or be angry at him. I love him and I love the family we are raising. I love our life," she continued.

"Francisco agreed to work at it with me, and we are seeing a counselor now. My husband is a nice guy, and I'm trying to understand what was going on in his head to do something like that. The thing is, culturally here, every other guy is cheating on his wife," Sonia said trying to put the whole issue in perspective.

"Francisco is surrounded by paparazzi and models because of his polo career, so I can understand him falling into a weak spot and going with the flow," she continued. "So we are working things out; some days are better than others, but we are figuring it out."

Lea could hear the acceptance in her friend's voice.

She knew this was harder on Sonia than she could admit, but she also knew that her friend would prioritize her children and her family life before her, and that if Francisco was willing to work at it, she would give him a chance.

"Make sure you are both working at this— not just you," Lea reminded her as they were saying good-bye. They had been talking for an hour now and Lea needed to take a shower before her kids came home.

"I will, Happy Thanksgiving," Sonia said as they hung up.

"Thank you, have a good weekend," Lea said. It was Wednesday before Thanksgiving, and the kids would be home around one in the afternoon. Lea knew Sonia did not celebrate Thanksgiving, as it is not a holiday celebrated in Argentina, but she remembered the many times Sonia had come home with her to celebrate with her family.

She remembered how much fun they had had, and how much Sonia had enjoyed the simplicity of a meal with her family, cooked by the family and served by the family. She had enjoyed being in the kitchen with her mum and her sisters learning how to use a knife, helping prep the stuffing, and make the pies. She had never been part of something like that, having been raised with multiple maids and a cook.

Lea also enjoyed this time of the year, and as her kids were getting older she enjoyed their help in the kitchen. She enjoyed their being part of the celebration and their helping to set the table and prepare the house.

When she finished her shower, she made herself some tea and sat at the kitchen table with a pile of cookbooks and family recipes. She had another half hour before the kids showed up. Some recipes were from her husband's family, some from her grandmother's. She was debating whether to prepare sweet potatoes or carrots as a side. As she picked up another recipe card from her recipe box, she heard a loud screech right outside her house.

She ran out the front door to see her son's bus right in front of her house and the driver jumping off the bus and screaming. Before she could fully understand what was going on, she saw her son's backpack on the ground and a blue minivan that had come from the opposite direction stopped there, as well.

She ran to the street and saw her son lying face down on the pavement. The driver was dialing 911 as the woman driving the minivan was kneeling next to her son holding her head.

Lea knelt down next to Colin, putting her hand on his neck to feel his breathing.

"Baby, it's Mummy, can you hear me?" she whispered next to her son's ear. His forehead had a cut. Lea could feel the hard wet pavement under her knees. She wanted to place her sweater under her son's face but she did not dare move him.

"Hmm," Lea heard her son muttering. Lea took off her outer layer and placed it on her son, talking to him as she did so. "Mummy is here, you will be all right. Hang in there baby, Mummy is here," she kept whispering as she felt completely useless seeing her son on the ground.

The ambulance came in what to Lea felt like days. Two paramedics rushed to her son's side; they stabilized his neck and lifted him onto a stretcher. Lea ran in the house to get her cell phone and then got into the ambulance with her son.

His eyes were open, staring into nothing. "Colin, can you hear me? It's Mummy. If you can hear me, please blink once," she said. The paramedic sitting next to her encouraged her to keep on talking to him.

Lea kept talking to Colin trying to comfort him, and finally he blinked once and she could see a soft smile.

"He can hear me," Lea said in relief.

She had managed to text both her husband and her neighbor as they drove the four miles that separated the house from the nearest hospital. The neighbor had answered immediately. She was going to wait in the house for the other two children to come home. Paul had not yet responded to her text.

"We are almost there," Lea said to Colin holding his hand as they made the last turn into the emergency room entrance of the large hospital.

Lea was shoved away as they wheeled Colin into the emergency room. A hospital staff member led Lea to a waiting room where she sat her down with a glass of water and asked Lea about her son: his age, his medical history, etc.

Lea felt like she was in a daze. She responded to the questioning mechanically, reciting information she had been asked hundreds of times before, whenever she took her children to the pediatrician.

"Have you communicated with your husband?" the woman asked Lea one more time, bringing Lea back into the room, into her reality.

"No, no, not yet. He has not responded to my text," Lea answered the woman asking her all these questions and who was now pointing to the cell phone clasped in her shaky hand.

"Can I have the number and I can try calling him?" she asked with a smile as Lea gave her the cell phone and the woman, expertly without prompting, went into Lea's list of contacts to find someone with her last name.

"Paul ... Is that his name?" the woman asked as Lea nodded, holding her head in her hands.

"Mrs. Garris?" a police officer came into the room and approached Lea.

"Yes?" Lea answered the officer.

"I would like to ask some questions about your son's accident," he said taking a seat next to Lea.

"Did you see it happen?" he asked pulling out a pad of paper and a pen.

"No, I did not. I was in the kitchen when I heard a loud screech of brakes. I ran to the street and that's when I... that's when I..." she kept repeating, as the image of her son's backpack brought her back to those first seconds.

"It's OK," the police officer said realizing that she was not able to continue. Lea had covered her face with her hands and was sobbing uncontrollably.

"What happened, where's Colin?" Paul said running into the waiting room. He had come in through the emergency room door and had been ushered to where his wife was waiting.

Lea was still in a daze, and tears were welling up in her eyes. "What happened, where is he?" Paul kept asking as he knelt in front of Lea.

A hospital staff member answered as Lea was not responding to her husband's questions. "He is being checked out in the emergency room unit, the doctors will be coming out any minute now."

"Are you Colin's parents?" a doctor said as both Lea and Paul looked up. The police officer had already left promising to contact them with more details of the accident.

"Yes," Lea and Paul both said at once.

"Is he going to be OK?" Lea asked with a shaky voice.

"He is stable right now. He had a pretty big trauma. We have stabilized him and he is resting, but his liver was badly hit. We have put his name on the list for a donor and we are waiting to see what is available right away. He will need a transplant in the next 48 to 72 hours," the doctor said plainly no emotion in his face.

"A transplant, but why, how is he, will he survive?" Lea's words were pouring out without much thinking. She was in shock. "Can I see him, can we stay with him?"

"Right now he is in the ICU being carefully monitored. We rather he is isolated for the moment so that we can observe how his body reacts to the trauma. We have managed to stop the internal bleeding and there is a slight chance that because he is young and healthy, the liver will heal itself but we won't know for sure until tomorrow. The next 24 hours are crucial," he continued as he excused himself to respond to a beeper attached to his waist.

"What happened?" Paul said now sitting next to Lea as the doctor walked out of the waiting room.

"I was in the kitchen when I heard a loud screech. I ran out of the house and saw Colin's backpack on the ground, and then saw him lying on the pavement. A blue minivan had stopped and a woman was screaming next to him, the bus driver was there too, it was all very confusing and then the ambulance came…" she said to her husband, her eyes glassy as she rambled on.

"I need to see Colin, I need to see him," she said as she shook from head to toe, her hands folded in front of her, her legs tightly crossed.

"I know, I know," Paul said as he hugged her and rested his head on her shoulder.

They held each other for hours, not noticing the passing of time, the room turning dark.

CHAPTER 15

"We should go home and make sure Lauren and Jenny are taken care of," Paul said after a while, releasing his wife and sitting next to her.

"I know, but I can't leave in case they need us. I need to stay with Colin," Lea said refusing to leave the hospital.

"I'll go home then. I'll make sure that Julie can keep them for the night and I'll bring some clothes for you and call our parents," Paul said feeling useful for the first time since he got to the hospital.

"OK," Lea said half listening.

Paul kissed her forehead as he spoke briefly to the staff at the desk before he left the waiting room and headed to his car.

When the girls got off their buses, their neighbor Julie was waiting for them at the bus stop. Paul drove straight to the neighbor's house; his house sat dark in the cold November night.

"Is that you, Paul?" Julie asked as Paul slowly opened the side door letting himself in. They had been neighbors with Julie and her husband for over seven years now and both families had always been there for each other. Julie's children were now grown and gone away from home. Julie always enjoyed watching Paul and Lea's kids when they needed to run an errand, but there had never been an emergency like this before.

"Yes, Julie, it's me. Thank you so much for your help," he said as he walked into the kitchen seeing his daughters at the kitchen table having dinner.

"Do you need some food?" she asked pouring soup into a deep bowl before Paul could answer.

"Oh, thank you," Paul said as he took a seat between his daughters and accepted the bowl of soup.

"What happened, Daddy? Where's Mommy?" Lauren asked looking at her father with worried eyes.

"Mommy is in the hospital with Colin," Paul began as he held his daughters' hands in his and controlled his emotion so as not to scare them.

"Colin had an accident. As he got off his bus, a car driving too fast did not stop as he was crossing the street and hit him," Paul explained.

"Is he dead?" Lauren asked as only an eight-year-old can ask, her eyes wide.

"No, he is not. He is very hurt though and the doctors are doing all they can to help him," he answered not over explaining but not hiding the truth either.

"Will he be OK?" Jenny asked in a whisper, speaking up for the first time since Paul walked into Julie's house.

"We don't know yet, but he is stable for now," he said looking at his older daughter with a sad smile and gently touching her cheek with the back of his hand in a sad gesture. He felt his daughter responding to his touch, her face gently tilting toward his hand as he pulled back his chair and let her sit on his lap. Lauren stood up as well and came close. He hugged his girls for what felt like hours but was just a short minute. Both girls cried on his shoulder and he allowed himself to slowly release his tears as Julie watched them from her place by the stove, her heart sinking at the sight of the embrace.

"Paul, don't worry about the girls. You go ahead and go back to the hospital to stay with Lea. The girls will stay with us and have Thanksgiving dinner here with my in-laws and some friends," Julie said stepping in as the three went back to their seats and to their soups, helping Paul figure out the next steps. She was walking Paul through the next few hours, helping her neighbor take it one step at a time.

"Thank you Julie. I'm going to the house now to get some clothes. If you girls want to come with me, you can get an overnight bag so that you have your things for the night," Paul said as he stood up, having finished his soup and grateful for something warm. "I'll also leave a set of keys so that you can go into the house with the girls at any time. We'll see how the night goes, but maybe we'll take the girls to the hospital tomorrow and we can have dinner there—we'll see. It's too early to know right now,"

It took Paul and the girls just ten minutes before they were back in Julie's kitchen. Lauren had brought her pillow and some bears and Jenny had helped her pack a change of clothes and pajamas. Jenny had a small bag with her book, her laptop, and a change of clothes.

"Here you go, please take this to Lea and don't worry about the girls. We will play games tonight or maybe watch a movie. Fred will be home late tonight so I will enjoy their company," Julie said giving Paul a small tote bag with a container of warm chicken soup, some fresh bread, a couple of apples, and some warm cookies as she ushered Paul toward the door.

"Thank you so much," Paul said as he hugged his girls who had also walked him to the door.

"Give this to Colin," Lauren said to Paul as she took off a thin gold necklace with a Silver Star charm. It had been her birthday gift. "It's a lucky star, it will protect him."

"Thank you, baby," Paul said hugging his younger daughter once more and fighting back tears.

"Tell Colin I love him," Jenny said tearfully as she hugged her father.

"I will. I'll see you tomorrow. Julie, Lea and I have our cell phones so call us or text us if you need anything," Paul said as Julie nodded and said that she could bring the girls to the hospital tomorrow at any time.

Paul got in his car and placed his bag and Julie's care package on the passenger seat. He backed out into the street and headed to the hospital. He called his parents, now in Florida for the winter, as he drove to the hospital.

"What happened?" his father said as his mother passed the phone. She had been too shocked to continue with the conversation.

"Colin is in the hospital. A car hit him as he got off the school bus. He might need a liver transplant," Paul said now sounding tired as he retold to his parents all he knew about the accident.

"Have you seen him, is Lea with you?" his father said as Paul passed the gas station and turned into the hospital general parking lot.

"Lea is at the hospital. I'm on my way back there now. I just came back to the house to make sure our neighbor was OK staying with the girls. No, I have not seen Colin yet," Paul said as he parked the car and took the bag and care package with him.

It was now pitch dark and the temperature was dropping. Paul could see his breath as he locked the car. He should have grabbed a jacket, but in the rush of packing for Lea he had forgotten. He clutched the bag against his chest as he hurried toward the emergency room entrance.

"My friend Dr. Stratts works at St. Luke's Hospital. I assume Colin is there, right? I'll give him a call as I know he works with a team for high-risk transplants," his father said.

Paul's father was always the solve-it-all kind of

person. He had been a doctor, now retired, and had been socially very active in their community for years. He knew everyone at the hospital.

"Thanks, Dad, that would be great. I have to go now, I'm walking back into the hospital," Paul said as the automatic doors opened in front of him. He hurried into the emergency room and then proceeded to the waiting room where he had left Lea.

"Call any time, son, and send our love to Lea and Colin. I won't tell the whole thing to your mother right now as you know she has a weak heart, but I'm here for whatever you need," he said as Paul thanked him and put away his phone. He had remembered to get both his and Lea's chargers so that they could plug in their phones while at the hospital.

Lea was nowhere to be found as he walked to where she had been sitting. He approached the staff woman at the desk.

"I'm here with Mrs. Garris. Our son Colin is in the emergency ICU," Paul said to the woman behind her desk. The shift had changed and the woman behind the counter was not the same person Paul had seen before. She was wearing light-blue scrubs and her dark hair was pulled tightly in a ponytail. She was probably in her mid-thirties, heavy set with a pretty face.

"Yes, Mr. Garris. Your wife was here until a few minutes ago, but she was just ushered in to your son's side. Apparently he woke up and was asking for both of you," she said with a wide smile. "I can show you in if you want."

"Thank you," Paul said, his heart racing with the anxiety of seeing his son for the first time since the accident.

He was shown into an anteroom where he was given a locker to put his clothes and stuff in before putting on a full scrub on top of his clothes. He put on a thin cap over his hair and covered his shoes with a special fabric cover.

With shaky hands Paul went through the open door as the woman announced him on an intercom.

In the ICU a nurse gave him a facemask, and he followed her into a room at the far end of the corridor. The place was silent but for the sound of low humming coming from different rooms. There were rooms on each side of the aisle as Paul made his way. Most of the doors were closed with doctors and nurses coming in and out of rooms carrying papers and a stethoscope around their necks.

The nurse stopped in front of room #8 and slowly opened the door to let Paul in. Lea was sitting on a chair next to Colin, holding his hand. His son seemed to be sleeping, but as he approached the bed and stood behind his wife Colin opened his eyes and gave a weak smile to his father.

"Hi, son," Paul managed to say as he placed his hand on top of his wife's and his son's, his other hand resting on Lea's shoulder.

"They let me in a few minutes ago," Lea said in a whisper. "He is not able to talk, but he squeezed my hand a few minutes ago. He has been given all kinds of stuff to slow his body down and keep him in a state of half-consciousness," she said as she sat there, relieved to have her husband with her.

"I brought you some dinner from Julie's. Why don't you go and have some soup— it's in my locker in the changing room. I'll stay with Colin for a few minutes. You need to eat something; it's going to be a long night," Paul said urging his wife to take care of herself.

Lea stood up and squeezed her husband's hand as she walked out of the room. Paul took a seat on Lea's chair and grabbed his son's hand in his.

"Colin, please be strong. You are so young and we love you so much," he said in a low soft voice to his son. He talked to his son like this for over twenty minutes while his wife was out of the room. He had read somewhere about the importance of family connecting to their loved ones in these kinds of situations and how patients even in a coma could still hear and feel their family around them urging them to fight, to stay strong.

"I remember when you were a little boy, you wanted a yellow ball you had seen at your friend's house. You were so stubborn about it, you wouldn't take no for an answer," Paul continued retelling anecdotes from Colin's childhood remembering every little detail of his childhood. "You kept crying for the ball and didn't want anything except that yellow ball. I think you were about four years old. Next thing we know, your mother and I were in the kitchen and we noticed that you were missing. You had left the house and walked the two blocks from our home and your friend's house. You knocked on the door and you, very politely, asked your friend's mother if you could borrow the yellow ball, just for a few days. The mother agreed and gave you the ball and your mother and I, who by now were frantically looking for you, found you walking back with a smile from ear to ear and the ball in your hands," Paul smiled as he remembered the story. "I want you to be that stubborn right now, my son. Focus on you and me playing and goofing around in the yard again, focus on going skiing this season," Paul said a tear rolling down his cheek.

He looked at his son who still lay with his eyes closed,

his chest rising rhythmically with each breath. The left side of his face had abrasions from his forehead to his chin. A white bandage over his eyebrow concealed the few stitches they had done on his left eyebrow.

A tube went in through his nose and down his throat to ensure the proper flow of oxygen. He had an oxygen mask over his mouth as well. His left arm was in a bandage while his right arm was stretched out, palm up, an IV secured at the nook of his elbow.

A thin white blanket covered Colin's body, but Paul could see the bulge of a brace on his left leg. His leg would need a cast eventually as he had broken his ankle but for now they had stabilized it with a brace.

Paul knew that the abrasions or the leg were not the real problem. These were all minor injuries. He knew enough to know that a Grade IV trauma in the liver was something that could take his son's life if his body did not heal itself a transplant was not found soon.

A doctor and a nurse came into the room and signaled for Paul to wait outside.

"Did you get the soup?" Paul asked as he met with Lea back in the waiting room.

"Yes, thank you," Lea said as the doctor came in to talk to them.

Lea and Paul stood up as he approached them.

"I just checked on your son," he said looking at Colin's chart. "He is stable, but at this point it looks like we will need to begin pursuing a transplant. There is a 20% chance that he might not need it if, as has happened before, the liver tissue begins regenerating itself. Unfortunately the trauma is so severe that there may not be enough time," the doctor explained.

"What are our options?" Lea asked with a clear, practical voice. "What can we do?"

"There have been cases when a live donor can donate a piece of their liver without any major consequences, as the liver does regenerate itself. It has been done but it's still not 100% safe. In the case of Colin …" he said looking down at his chart to make sure he got the name right. "If by tomorrow we confirm that he needs a transplant, he will need a full organ transplant, from a donor, a deceased donor," he continued looking at both Lea and Paul.

"Where do we get one? What is the procedure?" Lea asked without hesitation. She had her mother cap on and there was no emotion in her voice; that would come later. At this time she was focusing on the steps to follow for her son's recovery.

"We have already listed Colin on the national waiting list as an emergency case. Because of his age and the circumstances and knowing that he would have very high chances of full recovery with an organ transplant, his name is at the top of the list. The problem is that it needs to be a local donor for us to be able to access this organ within the time frame that we need for him to survive," the doctor explained.

"I would suggest that you go home and we will call you if anything changes overnight. Or you can stay here if you choose. You can be with your son every hour for about ten minutes, just try to not wake him up. We are keeping him in as low a dose as we can of anesthesia for the pain. The more he sleeps the better it is," he said as he excused himself and walked back into the ICU.

"I'm not going anywhere," Lea said as soon as the doctor left.

"I know. We don't need to. The girls are well taken care of. We will stay here and take turns going in to be with Colin," Paul said as he took a seat next to his wife and held her hand.

"I just can't believe we are here," Lea said, her free hand on her face.

"It seems so surreal. I was just going through the recipes for Thanksgiving. It was an ordinary day; I just can't believe this happened," Lea kept saying going over the whole day in her head.

Paul patted her hand and leaned back on his chair.

It was a long night for both of them. They took turns going in to see their son every hour on the hour.

Paul a heavy coffee drinker by nature kept going to the end of the corridor to refill his coffee mug.

At around 3 AM they heard a rush of activity in the emergency room entrance and a woman in her forties walked into the waiting room clutching a purse and a man's sport coat.

She took a seat at the other end of the room, staring into space.

A doctor came about a half hour later and had a quiet conversation with the woman before he left her there again.

She sat down and stayed there, not moving.

"Would you like some coffee?" Paul asked the newcomer approaching her as he was heading to refill his mug again.

"Oh, thank you. Yes, thank you," she said a little bit surprised by his question.

The family waiting room was not staffed during the night. If you needed to talk to anyone, you had to go out into the emergency room lobby where a nurse manned the reception desk.

"Here you go," Paul said as he handed the woman a coffee cup and some sugar packages.

"Thank you," she said. She was wearing a pair of jeans, leather boots, and a gray turtleneck. Her blond hair was pulled back in a bun. She had bright blue eyes and she was tall, probably taller than Lea who was five foot seven. Her English had a slight accent Lea noticed, and she tried to figure out where she had heard that accent before.

Paul wanted to talk to the woman, to ask why she was there, but he stayed by Lea's side. As five o'clock came around, Lea walked to the ICU room for her turn to see her son.

"Do you have someone in the emergency room?" Paul asked taking a seat next to the woman.

"Yes, my brother," she said looking at Paul.

"Sorry, my name is Paul," he said extending his hand as he introduced himself.

"Julia, Julia von Bearb," she said as she shook Paul's hand.

"Who are you here for?" she asked Paul seeing that his wife was here with him and assuming it was probably one of their parents or an elderly relative.

"My son, Colin. He's thirteen. A car hit him as he got off his school bus right in front of our home," Paul said as he clenched his hands around his coffee mug.

"I'm so sorry, hope he's OK," she said.

"Is your brother going to be all right?" Paul asked trying to think of something else other than why he was there talking to a stranger at five in the morning on Thanksgiving Day.

"He had a stroke. An aneurism," she said. "He is visiting for the holidays. We had gone out to dinner and then went to bed. I heard him getting up in the middle of the night and he was sick in the bathroom. I got up, assuming he had eaten something that did not sit well with him, and I found him passed out on the bathroom floor. My husband called 911 and I rode in the ambulance with him. He is only thirty-nine," she said rubbing her eyes with the back of her right hand as her left hand rested on her knee holding the coffee cup.

"I'm sorry," Paul said as the door opened and his wife came into the waiting room. Lea had tears in her eyes as she went to her husband.

"He is in pain," she said as Paul took her into his arms. "He looked at me and he had tears running down his cheeks," Lea said as she sobbed into her husband's arms.

"He will be OK. The doctor is right there. Should I talk to him?" Paul asked, trying desperately to fix it, whatever it was, he wanted to fix it.

"The doctor came in as I was leaving. The nurse said they were going to give him more pain medicine just to make him comfortable," Lea said.

"Why don't you go home and maybe sleep for an hour or two and then come back?" Paul said hoping his wife would agree to leave for a few hours. She looked exhausted and he knew they were in for a long day and a few very long nights.

"I can call a taxi to get you home," he said as she surprisingly agreed to go home.

Lea took a taxi straight home; Paul had to give her keys to the house, as she did not even bring her house keys when she had left the house the afternoon of the accident.

It was only five-thirty in the morning so she didn't go to her neighbor's to see her daughters; she went into the house and straight up to Colin's room. Julia had come earlier and taken Missy their dog to her house as well, so Lea was all alone in the house.

Without even taking her shoes off, Lea collapsed onto Colin's bed crying into his pillow. Her hair was sticking to her face as she lay on the mattress with her clenched fists and cried herself to sleep.

"Mom, is that you?" came the voice of Jenny as she

walked up the stairs.

Lea awoke with a start. At first she did not know where she was, but then the events of the last twenty-four hours came back to her in waves and she realized she was on her son's bed.

"I'm here," she said with a cracked voice to direct Jenny to where she was.

She sat up on Colin's bed and dried her face with her sleeve. The sun was up but she had no idea what time it was.

"What are you doing here?" Jenny asked walking toward her mother, and noticing Lea's puffy eyes and red nose. She sat on the bed and hugged her mother for what Lea thought was the first time her oldest daughter took the initiative to connect with her emotionally.

"How is Colin?" Jenny asked releasing her mother and looking at her straight in the eyes.

"Is Lauren here with you?" Lea asked looking toward the open door.

"No, she is at Julie's. I came in to grab hats and gloves as it's cold and we are heading out for a walk," Jenny said.

"He is not good. His liver is not working well; he got hit pretty hard and it's likely he might need a transplant. Jenny, it's very scary," Lea said allowing her tears to flow again and opening up to her daughter.

"Will he be OK?" Jenny asked tears now rolling down her face as she asked in a whisper. Although she was old enough to get the full story, she only wanted to know the end result. She only wanted to know if her brother would be OK.

"I hope so. I pray so, but we don't know yet, honey," Lea said as she hugged her daughter.

"What time is it?" Lea asked looking around her son's room for an alarm clock or something to tell her the time.

"It's about nine-thirty," Jenny said as Lea rose from the bed.

"Oh my god, I need to get back to the hospital. I can't believe I slept this much. Let Julie know that I was here for a few hours. I'm going to take a quick shower and then go back to the hospital. Jenny, please help with Lauren. We will call you later to let you know how things are going. Maybe Daddy will come home in a couple of hours; we just don't know yet how the day is going to go," Lea said as she hurried out of the room to her bedroom, giving her daughter a hug on the way.

"OK," Jenny said as she ran down the stairs and back

to their neighbor's house.

Lea rushed through her shower and changed into comfortable jeans, a turtleneck, and a cardigan. She put on warm comfortable socks and her UGG boots.

Grabbing a tote bag from the linen closet she grabbed some books for herself and Paul, then put in Colin's iPod touch. In his closet she found his favorite stuffed animal from childhood, a now ragged dinosaur Colin had slept with for years from the time he was about four years old.

From the kitchen she grabbed and filled a couple of reusable water bottles, a couple of granola bars, and some fruit.

As she got into her car she checked her cell phone. She had two new text messages.

"Are u on ur way back?" was the first message from Paul at around 9 AM.

"Where are u?" was the second message at 9:30 AM.

It was now almost 10:30 and her heart was racing as she got into the car and reversed out of her garage as she called her husband.

"What happened?" Lea said as soon as her husband picked up. She maneuvered her car out into the street balancing the phone between her shoulder and her ear.

"Where are you?" Paul. She could hear the anxiety in his voice.

"I'm leaving the house right now. I'll be there in ten minutes. Is Colin OK?" she asked as she took a turn in the direction of the hospital.

"We can talk when you get here. Colin is fine, no change yet," Paul said reassuring Lea that their son was fine but not totally convincing Lea.

She pulled into the emergency room parking lot and rushed into the building.

"What happened?" were her first words as she entered the waiting room where Paul, sat looking tired and disheveled, his head down and his hands clasped in front of him, his elbows on his knees.

There was nobody else in the waiting room other than her husband. Nobody was at the desk, and the lady Lea had seen earlier that morning was no longer there.

"Colin needs a transplant; it's confirmed. His body is not able to react positively right now, and he is now fully intubated to allow his body to function," he said slowly in a whisper. Working hard to pronounce each word, his full attention on getting the message out, putting all his energy in staying calm and collected in spite of his exhaustion and his emotional drain.

"Oh my god," Lea said sitting next to Paul, dropping her jacket and bag on the floor and covering her face with her hands.

"The good news though," Paul continued, as Lea looked up to him and wondered what on earth could be the good news.

"The good news is that they might have already found a donor for him. Do you remember the woman that came in late last night?" Lea nodded remembering the tall blond woman that walked in at around 3 AM the night before.

"Her brother is now in a coma. He had a stroke last night and he is completely brain dead. He had signed a will that if he was ever in that situation his wish was that they would harvest his organs. They have already run tests and he is compatible with Colin. He would be a good match and his body is in good shape for his age," Paul said matter of fact, giving Lea all the technical information in the same way the doctors had given it to him an hour ago. He had no emotion for the dying man; he was only focused on what was needed for his son to live.

"That is great. I feel so sorry for the family," Lea said as she listened to her husband, hopeful for the first time in the last 24 hours.

"Is he married, does he have kids?" Lea said as the

reality of someone dying for her son to live, hit her.

"No, he is single. He was visiting his sister who lives locally. They are from Europe, Austria I think," Paul said, as Lea opened the bag and grabbed some fruit and water for her husband.

That was strange, she was reminded of the new friend she had made in Costa Rica, also from Austria. She had rarely met people from that country and now two of them had come into her life just in the last month.

Paul had gone to clean himself up in the public restroom using the toiletries Lea had brought, he returned to Lea in the family room.

A doctor came in to the family room and addressed Lea. "Mrs. Garris?"

"Yes?" she said standing up to meet the doctor halfway.

"Did your husband explain to you the situation as it stands right now?" the doctor asked as Lea nodded. "We have run enough tests to know that the donor is a good match for your son. His family is flying in from Europe this afternoon, and once the appropriate amount of time has gone by we will be able to harvest his organs. We have started to prepare Colin for the procedure with medications that will enable his body to accept the organ," he continued as Lea tried to retain everything he was saying.

"Mrs. Garris, you understand how lucky your son has been? We were getting ready to wait for days if not weeks for a donor, every day reducing the chances of your son living, as his body deteriorates with the lack of a functioning liver. There's only so much we can do to keep him alive," he said as he walked back to the ICU.

"I understand," Lea said not necessarily thinking herself lucky for even being in this situation.

"Can I come in to see him?" she asked before the doctor disappeared through the doors.

"We will come get you in an hour or so. Right now we are monitoring him closely as we give him some new medication," he said scanning his badge so that the doors would open.

Lea took a seat and waited for Paul to come back from the bathroom.

Pulling her phone from her pocket she began typing on the touch screen:

"Colin is in the hospital. Got hit by a car. Awaiting liver transplant. We found a donor. Girls are with Julie. Paul and I at the hospital."

She texted her mother, her sisters, her friend Sonia, and her friend Kara.

Lea and Paul visited Colin one more time that

morning before driving back to their house. The doctors had assured them he was stable. When Lea called Julie, she convinced them to join them for Thanksgiving dinner at her house.

Paul stopped at their house first to change; Lea went straight to her neighbor's house where Julie greeted her with a comforting hug as soon as she walked in. Lea allowed herself to relax into her friend's embrace.

"Mummy, Mummy," Lauren ran over to Lea as soon as she heard her voice; she hugged her tightly around her waist.

"Hello, baby," Lea said with a tired voice as she picked up her daughter and placed her on her hip. "You are getting too big for this," Lea said as she nuzzled her little girl's' nose with hers.

"How's Colin?" were Jenny's first words as they walked into the kitchen.

"He is hanging in there. He is a strong boy," Lea said with a sad smile.

"Dinner is served," Julie said as she ushered everyone to a beautifully laid table.

Julie's son was visiting with his brand-new wife who was expecting their first child.

Paul walked in as they started to seat themselves. The large oval table was decorated with flowers, mini pumpkins, and orange and mustard-colored napkins over a white starched tablecloth. She had lit candles on both the table and the buffet side table where the holiday spread was laid out.

There was turkey, mashed potatoes, green beans, gravy, stuffing, and a sweet potato casserole.

Lea and Paul sat as their daughters filled their plates and then sat in between the two of them at the large table. Lea forced herself to eat and be present for her girls even though her stomach was turning at the thought of her son lying in a hospital bed not far from them.

"We are thankful for friends and family around us. And we are thankful for hope and for Colin's recovery," Julie said raising her glass as everyone did the same around the table.

Lea swallowed her tears as she raised her own glass and forced a sad smile.

Julie knew about the transplant and the donor; she and Lea had been able to have a little conversation when the girls were helping bring the food into the dining room.

Paul had second servings but Lea barely finished her plate. They both got the food and company they needed for another sleepless night. Lea felt uncomfortable taking so much time away from the hospital, but she knew that the doctors would call her or Paul if there were any reason at all.

"Lea, the girls are going to stay with us again tonight. We have plans to go ice skating in Providence tomorrow and we are hoping they can join us," Julie said, as Lea and Paul got ready to go.

"Thank you so much, Julie. My mom just texted me this afternoon. She and my sister are flying over tomorrow so they will be able to take care of the girls and stay at our house. Paul and I are taking it day by day. We'll see when the transplant happens and how Colin reacts to it," Lea said hugging her friend as Paul hugged their daughters good-bye.

"Be good girls, and we will see you tomorrow. If you need to talk to us, just call our cell phones," Paul said to both his daughters as Lea hugged them.

Paul and Lea drove back to the hospital in silence, each of them reserving their energy for the night ahead.

As they walked into the waiting room, they saw a senior couple and the tall woman who had been with them the previous night.

They nodded in greeting as Lea and Paul took seats on the other side of the room. Lea wondered if they knew that their loved one would be donating one of his organs to her son. She supposed they didn't.

These things were usually kept anonymous.

"Mr. and Mrs. Garris?" the nurse came in walking straight to them.

"Yes?" they said in unison.

"You can come in now," the nurse said as she scanned her badge and ushered them into the anteroom where Lea and Paul now, knowing the routine, changed into the high hygienic clothing that they needed to enter the ICU.

Colin was laying just the way Lea and Paul had last seen him. The light in his room was turned off; only the dim outside lights illuminated her son as he lay still on his hospital bed. It was past four o'clock now and the sun was setting. He had now been in the hospital for twenty-four hours. —Twenty-four hours since he had last been walking around, a healthy happy thirteen years old.

Lea and Paul sat on each side of the bed. Lea gently rubbed Colin's left hand.

His face was pale and his lips were chapped under the oxygen mask. Paul ran his fingers through his son's hair feeling some remnants of dried blood around his left temple. Colin stirred; he felt his father's touch.

They sat with him for an hour or so. Lea saw people walking past her son's room through the half-open door. She saw the older couple that had been in the waiting room, the well-dressed woman hunched back, her hand on her face while the man who Lea assumed was her husband held her by the shoulders as he guided her to the exit of the ICU.

Lea suspected the man with the seizure must have been in the room next to her son's.

A couple of nurses came into the room to check on Colin, writing notes on the clipboard at the end of her son's bed. He slept.

Back in the waiting room two doctors updated Paul and Lea. "We are scheduling the transplant for tomorrow afternoon." Lea noticed that Dr. Merck, the doctor who had treated Colin yesterday afternoon, was still there looking tired with a day-old scrub growing.

"Dr. Botling will take over for me as I finish my shift," Dr. Merck said introducing the new doctor in charge. "I will be back tomorrow afternoon and the transplant is scheduled for five o'clock. We are getting a team together that will work with me in surgery," he said his voice reflecting the long shift he was now ending.

"Thank you," Lea said holding on to Paul's hand. She suspected this doctor had done a longer shift than normal just to look after her son.

"I suggest you sleep tonight. Colin is stable and he will be well taken care of. Tomorrow night will be a very long night. You should plan on being around after the surgery for at least twelve hours. If there are any complications, that's when they will happen," Dr. Merck said as he finished writing some notes on Colin's chart, which he handed to Dr. Botling.

It was now eight o'clock and Lea and Paul took a seat again in the waiting room evaluating what to do. They discussed whether they should both go home now and sleep or if one of them should stay while the other slept. The tall woman they had been with the night before and the older couple came into the waiting room. Their faces revealed their suffering.

As they sat a nurse approached them.

"Mr. and Mrs. Von Bearb?" the nurse asked as the couple stood up to meet her.

Lea looked up immediately. It couldn't be she thought. It must be a coincidence.

"Yes," Mr. and Mrs. Von Bearb said standing up to talk to the nurse.

"According to your son's will, he wished to donate his organs," the nurse said showing them some forms for them to sign. "Yes, we are aware of that," Mr. Von Bearb said with a strong accent reminding Lea of Alex, who she had met at the yoga center less than two weeks before.

The sound of Mr. Von Bearb's voice brought Lea to a faraway place, a place she had almost forgotten she had been to. In just two days her life had changed so much she barely remembered ever being in Costa Rica.

When the nurse left the room Lea could not hold back and approached the trio. She needed to know.

"Excuse me," she said approaching the older couple. They looked up. Mrs. Von Bearb was clutching a handkerchief, her eyes red and swollen. Lea could tell that in spite of her swollen eyes and tired expression she was a beautiful woman; she had Alex's eyes.

"Yes?" Mr. Von Bearb asked surprised by Lea's presence.

"Are you related to Alex von Bearb?" she asked bluntly, something told her she was right but she needed to know.

The couple and the woman looked at each other wondering who Lea was.

"Alex von Bearb is my son," Mr. Von Bearb said as he stood up and looked at Lea in the eyes.

Lea brought a hand to her mouth in shock.

"Is he...?" Lea could not finish the question but

pointed to the doors leading to the ICU.

Mr. Von Bearb nodded. "He had a seizure last night and is in a coma. There is nothing they can do for him," the tall woman said standing next to her father. "My name is Christle von Bearb. I'm Alex's sister," Christle said extending her hand to Lea. "Did you know my brother?"

Lea's eyes filled with tears and she could not say a word. She nodded to Alex's sister and then excused herself and ran to the restroom. By now, Paul, who at first was not sure why Lea was talking to the trio, had come toward them and just stood there as he saw his wife run out of the room.

"What happened?" Paul asked Christle trying to understand what had just taken place.

"Apparently your wife knows my brother," Christle said with a puzzled expression.

"Excuse me please," Paul said leaving Mr. Von Bearb and his daughter standing as he walked out of the room to go find his wife.

He found Lea pacing the corridor in front of the restroom, drying her eyes with the back of her sleeve and shaking her head as she walked back and forth aimlessly.

"What happened, what's going on?" Paul asked as he

stood in front of Lea and grabbed her by the shoulders forcing her to stop pacing back and forth.

"That man… that man," Lea said stuttering, shaking from head to toe.

"What about him?" Paul said trying to make sense of his wife's reaction.

"I just met him in Costa Rica, at the yoga center," Lea said managing a whole sentence and looking Paul straight in the eyes as tears poured down her cheeks.

"Two weeks ago, or whenever that was?" Paul asked surprised by the coincidence.

"Yes, I met him. I didn't just meet him, I spent time with him, and he became sort of my guide… He was a healer and a spiritual guide. He helped me so much during my stay. He was wonderful," Lea said maybe revealing too much to her husband all at once but not being able to help it. He let go of his grip and she began pacing back and forth again, shaking her head, too shocked to make sense of it all.

It took Lea a good twenty minutes before she composed herself and walked back into the waiting room.

Alex's parents and his sister were still seated where she had left them.

"Excuse my behavior," Lea said going to them as she

walked into the room and bent down in front of the small family, one knee on the floor.

"I met your son only two weeks ago, at a yoga center in Costa Rica. I thought he lived in New York but traveled most of the time. What was he doing here?" she asked speaking slowly, aware that maybe their English was not as good as Alex's.

"He did live in New York but he traveled all over the world giving lectures and conferences. He was staying with me over Thanksgiving. My husband and I live in Westport, and he had come to stay with us for the first time. He is usually out of the country this time of year," Alex's sister explained as the mother looked at both her daughter and her husband trying to make sense of the conversation. She obviously did not speak much English.

Alex's sister translated the conversation into German for her.

"Excuse me, my parents are from Vienna. We are Austrian, and my mother does not speak English," Christle explained switching back to English.

"I'm sorry but I'm in shock. I enjoyed meeting Alex very much, and we had agreed to stay in touch. I just can't believe what happened," Lea said again trying to make sense of it all.

"Do you have a family member in the ICU?" Alex's

sister asked now trying to make conversation; Lea's reaction was starting to upset her mother. Paul had now joined the group and was standing next to his wife.

"Yes, my son got hit by a minivan Wednesday as he got off the school bus; he is only thirteen," Lea said her eyes welling up again as she reminded herself of the reason she was standing there, in that waiting room, on a late Thursday evening, Thanksgiving day.

"I'm so sorry. Will he be OK?" Christle asked as her father and her mother left the waiting room in search of some food and a cup of coffee.

"Yes, well we hope so, he needs a…" Lea could not finish the sentence. All the pieces of the puzzle were now falling into place.

"Oh my god, your brother, Alex …" Lea said bringing her hand to her mouth one more time.

"Transplant?" Christle said understanding Lea's reaction. "Your son needs a transplant? So he is the first receiver of my brother's organs?"

Lea nodded.

"That's what he wanted. That's what he spent his life doing, bringing life to the darkest corners, bringing hope to people in pain, bringing peace to people suffering. Bringing life to your son is his ultimate gesture of the way he led his life," Christle said her voice breaking through her tears.

Lea looked at this woman for what seemed a long time. She was taller than her and she had Alex's eyes. Her hair was lighter and she was slim just like her brother.

Without a word the two women hugged each other; two strangers melting into a painful embrace, crying into each other's shoulders. Christle was crying for the loss of her dear and only brother and the life of the thirteen-year-old that was pending waiting for her brother's organ. Lea was crying for the loss of a friend, someone that in a short time had helped her to see not only the beauty in herself but the beauty in her life and had encouraged her to embrace and protect her family, in spite of her feelings for him; and for her dear son whose life depended on his generosity and his tragedy.

Paul just watched the whole scene his mouth open in surprise. He had never heard of this Alex; Lea had not said much about her trip anyway. He was surprised, maybe jealous, sad for him and his family and grateful for this miracle for his son, all at the same time.

"Excuse me. I need to look for my parents. They flew in from Europe this morning and they are very tired. It's been a shock for them. Alex was their only son;

they now only have me," Christle said excusing herself and leaving the room.

Lea took a seat next to Paul and explained to him how she had met Alex, how he had been in the van with them from the airport, and how he had helped them with their bags. She told him about his constant attentiveness to her during the week there, how he helped her reconnect with herself, and how he had helped her find the beauty in the small things. She had not known at the time that he was a healer and spiritual speaker. She was honest with her husband not trying to conceal how close she and Alex had become in a very short period of time. Paul just listened and held her hand.

That night they spent at their house. By the time they got there it was close to ten o'clock; they did not bother disturbing the girls who were still sleeping at Julie's. Lea's mother was arriving the next day and she would take care of everything.

Paul and Lea slept next to each other for the first time in two days, they barely managed to get their clothes off before they collapsed on the bed falling asleep instantly. They fell asleep holding hands.

The doctor had told them that there was nothing for them to do before noon and that they would be able to spend an hour or so with Colin then, before he was moved to the surgical floor where they would prepare him for the transplant. All the tests had been done and the fact that the donor was still on life support at the same hospital made the doctors very confident of the results of the procedure as the organ was going to go from the donor to their son within minutes from harvesting.

Lea showered and changed, her heart heavy with anticipation of her son's surgery and the loss of her friend.

She had a restless sleep. Playing over and over in her head was that moment on the beach when her hands connected with Alex

"Mum, Colin is having his transplant this afternoon. When are you coming?" Lea asked as she talked to her mother on her cell phone, while Paul poured coffee for both of them and joined her at the kitchen table where they were having breakfast before heading back to the hospital. It was now eleven in the morning.

"OK, the girls will be waiting for you at Julie's. They have keys to the house. I'll call you as soon as the surgery is over; it might be very late though," Lea said as she finished her conversation and hung up.

"When are they coming?" Paul asked as he poured himself a bowl of cereal and milk.

"Mum and Cynthia will be landing in Logan at three

so they should be getting the girls around five this afternoon," Lea said as she texted this information to both her daughter Jenny and Julie.

It was now Friday after Thanksgiving, Black Friday, and the road to the hospital, which was located just down the road from the main shopping center, was heavy with shopping traffic. It took them over twenty minutes to make the trip that usually took ten minutes

"This is insane," Paul complained banging the palms of his hands on the steering wheel. "I've never seen this many people heading to the mall. This whole thing of a shopping binge after Thanksgiving is getting out of control; each year is worse. "

They were both at wit's end. They had not mentioned Colin all morning other than Lea's conversation with her mother. They almost had a silent pact between them, the less they talked about it, the less they reminded each other, and the better they were.

The waiting room was deserted when they got to the hospital but the emergency room lobby was busy with people coming in and going out. Some had minor cuts, others had food poisoning or other minor issues.

Lea and Paul sat in their regular corner and at 12 o'clock a nurse came out looking for them.

"You can come in now," she said escorting them back to see their son.

Nothing had really changed other than it seemed like they had moved some of the IVs on Colin's arm and Lea noticed that there were fresh dressing on his wounds on his left arm and face.

As they approached the bed, Colin opened his eyes. He still could not talk as he still had the breathing tube and the breathing mask. He turned to look at his mother and then at his father.

Lea grabbed his hand and her son responded to her touch. She smiled as she allowed a tear to roll down her cheek.

"Everything will be all right," Lea said soothingly whispering into her son's ear. "You are having surgery this afternoon which will help you with the pain."

Paul stood behind Lea and watched his son. His heart was heavy but he was relieved to see his son awake and responding to them.

"Lauren sends you this," Lea said taking the star charm from around her neck and showing it to her son. "She said it was her lucky star and that it would bring you luck," Lea said as she placed the star in her son's hand letting him feel it. Paul had given it to her.

There was movement across the hall and Lea looked up through the open door. Mr. and Mrs. Von Bearb were walking down the corridor, their daughter behind them. Lea could hear Mrs. Von Bearb's loud sobs as two nurses walked with them to the door ready for action if any of them needed any assistance.

"I'll be right back," Lea said turning to Paul and squeezing her son's hand as she walked out of the room.

She saw a nurse in the corridor and asked her if she could go into Alex's room. Lea was surprised when the nurse allowed her to go in.

She tiptoed into the room; he was lying on the bed, his body connected to multiple machines that were beeping in the background. His chest moved up and down as a machine artificially forced his lungs to inhale and exhale.

His face was just as Lea had remembered. He even had the tan she had first noticed on him.

Walking to the side of his bed she touched his hand; it was cold.

"Thank you," she whispered knowing that he probably could not hear her but not willing to believe it.

"Thank you for coming into my life, thank you for spending a week with me, and for showing me the beauty in this world. Thank you for giving life to my son," she said allowing her tears to flow, dripping on to the bed and on to his hand.

Lifting his hand slightly she placed her palm on his palm, mimicking their connection on that beach only a few weeks ago. The heat she had felt from his hand was no longer there. She felt her energy flowing from her to him, but she did not feel any energy coming from him. She closed her eyes and took a deep breath as she allowed the palm of her hand to feel her friend's.

"Good-bye, Alex. Namaste," she said as she leaned over and kissed his forehead.

She walked out of the room feeling a sense of peace and relief as she had not felt for days now. She was smiling.

Paul met her outside of the room and walked with her toward the exit. It was now time for them to let the doctors prepare Colin for the procedure. Both Alex and Colin would be moved to the fourth floor where the high-risk surgeries took place. There was another young boy in a similar situation as Colin's that would receive an organ from Alex that same evening.

Lea and Paul sat in the cafeteria, the dinner tray in front of them. Lea could barely take a sip of her soup while Paul managed to finish a whole cheeseburger and fries.

"They say that if it all goes well, Colin should be able to go home in about a week," Lea said as she played with her food. "He would have to stay home from school for at least a few weeks after that but not much more than that."

"Hmm, that's good," Paul said between mouthfuls.

"Should we go away for Christmas?" Lea said focusing her mind on a successful ending to this horrible week. "I think we will need to regroup as a family after this one."

"Where would you want to go?" Paul asked joining his wife in looking into the future with a positive attitude.

"I don't know. Somewhere warm. Colin will be too weak to do any sports and I would like a place where we can relax as a family. Maybe we should join your parents in Florida? We can get an apartment on the beach near their house," Lea said as the possibility of spending time with all her children in a relaxed atmosphere began to take hold and she pictured it in her mind as the best option for the week they were hoping to end soon.

"We can talk about it," Paul said as he wiped his mouth with a napkin and took a sip of his soda.

"Mr. and Mrs. Garris," the loudspeaker said surprising Lea and Paul who left the cafeteria without much hesitation, their food trays still on the table. Lea's food was barely touched.

They rushed to the fourth floor, their hearts racing. It was only nine o'clock. The doctors had told them that they would not be done before midnight.

"We are Mr. and Mrs. Garris," they both said short of breath as they raced from the elevator to the nurse's station on the fourth floor.

"Our son Colin is in surgery— they just called our names," Paul said trying to make sense for the nurse who regarded them with a puzzled look.

"Don't worry, everything is OK. You are Colin's parents, right?" the nurse asked reassuring them that there was no emergency.

"The doctor wants to talk to you, everything is OK, please follow me this way," the nurse said coming around her station and ushering Paul and Lea to a family waiting room at the end of the corridor.

It was a small room painted pale yellow. They seated themselves. There were only four or six chairs arranged around the room. A flat-screen TV in the far corner played the news with subtitles, the sound muted.

"Hello, please stay seated," Dr. Merck said as he walked in and sat on one of the chairs facing Paul and Lea.

"Everything is going well. The worst has passed. We

have successfully transplanted the organ, and we are now observing it before we finish the surgery. It was a perfect match, a miracle I must say. I've been a surgeon for over twenty years and I've never seen a better match and a better overall situation as this one. You should be thankful for this," he said as Lea closed her eyes tears rolling down her cheeks.

Her son would live, her friend was gone.

"We will probably finish with the surgery in about an hour or so. He will stay in the recovery room on this floor for the night, and tomorrow morning if he is doing well we will move him to a surgical recovery room on the sixth floor. By then he should only have a breathing tube and an IV for maybe a day or two, and he will be getting stronger and stronger by the hour. He is a strong healthy boy," the doctor said with a smile.

"The donor ... is he gone?" Lea asked with a shaky voice.

"Yes, he is. Luckily there were local patients waiting for organs so we have been able to successfully harvest the donor to its maximum potential. He will live through the lives he has enabled," the doctor said recognizing Lea's concern and being tactful about his comments, keeping the technicalities to a minimum.

"Thank you," Lea whispered. When the doctor left

them, Paul kneeled in front of his wife and took her in his arms rocking her as she cried, relieved by the good news, heartbroken about the loss of this kind stranger that was now part of their family forever, part of their son.

CHAPTER 16

"Let me see, let me see," Lauren said jumping up and down in excitement as her sister slowly opened a bright red package from under the tree.

"Thank you, Mum, Dad," Jenny said jumping to her feet and hugging her parents.

"You mean Santa Claus, right?" Lauren corrected her with a puzzled look.

"Yes, but Mum and Dad mailed my letter," Jenny said winking an eye to her parents as she patted Lauren on the head.

"This is so cool," Colin said as he opened his gift.

"Let me see, let me see," Lauren said running to him.

"I can't believe you got an iPad. I wanted one," she said pouting and looking at her parents.

"Well, maybe you need to open your present now," Lea said kneeling down and reaching under the tree for her daughter's gift. It was a large rectangular box wrapped in red and silver.

"What is it, what is it?" she asked as she grabbed the package from her mother and sat on the floor undoing the silver ribbon and tearing away the paper.

"I knew it, I've been asking for this for years, it's my own American Girl Doll," Lauren said grabbing the holiday-dressed doll and dancing around the living room. "Now I can go to the tea parties with my friends and have my own doll. I won't have to share other people's dolls."

Lea and Paul smiled at each other.

"And this is for you," Paul said giving Lea a small red box with a big gold bow on top.

"What is it, what is it?" Lea said mimicking her younger daughter.

"I don't know—you will have to open it. Were you a good girl this year?" Paul asked as he winked an eye to Colin and Jenny who were anxiously waiting for their mother to open the box.

"It's beautiful," Lea said as she pulled out a silver necklace with a charm star.

"And this is for you, and you, and you," Paul said as he gave identical boxes to Colin, Lauren, and Jenny.

As they each opened their boxes, they realized that they had all received an identical star charm. Jenny and Lauren's were just like their mother's and Colin's was hanging from a leather string instead of a silver chain.

"I don't want anyone ever forgetting how lucky we are," Paul said as Lea came and kissed him gently on the lips, a tear rolling down her cheek.

"Who's hungry?" a voice from the kitchen made them all look up to see their grandmother bringing in a plate full of muffins.

"We are!" the three kids said at once as they followed their grandmother to the outdoor deck.

"This was a good idea," Paul said taking Lea in his arms and kissing her.

Colin had recovered wonderfully from his surgery, and within two weeks he was himself again. While he still had to watch that he did not get overtired, he was pretty much back to a normal life.

Once they knew that Colin was ready to travel, they had booked a flight and gone to Paul's parents' house in Florida to spend the holidays. The house was roomy enough so that they did not need to rent another apartment. It was located right on the ocean in West Palm Beach, and Lea and Paul's bedroom on the second floor faced the beach, with the rhythmical sound of the ocean lulling them to sleep.

The three kids were inseparable. Jenny was attentive and careful with Colin at all times, and Lauren was in heaven pampered by her two older siblings.

Lea and Paul went for long walks on the beach every evening, holding hands and behaving like newlyweds. It was a time to rediscover each other. At night they slept in each other's arms. They enjoyed the warm weather and rejoiced as they watched their son recover his strength.

Lea still thought of Alex and felt the sadness of his loss, but somehow she could feel his presence through her son's smile.

Lea's mother had been very helpful the days that Colin was in the hospital, and she and her sister had managed to keep the girls busy and entertained while she and Paul focused on Colin. He had stayed in the hospital for a week so Lea and Paul had taken turns spending the nights on the cot next to him until he was released.

Sonia had been calling and texting Lea from the

moment she found out about Colin's accident, and she had sent a huge "Welcome home" basket with flowers, treats, movies, books, everything for Colin and the family when he was released from the hospital.

Lea's experience had further convinced Sonia that life was too short to not forgive her husband, and they seemed to be doing well, having so far survived their crisis and spending their holiday season in Punta del Este with the rest of their family.

Lea had not seen Alex's family after that last day at the hospital, when she saw them leaving the ICU, but she had been able to get the mailing address for Alex's sister and had sent a long and heartfelt letter to her and her parents praising their wonderful son and how his open heart and kindness had changed her life not once but twice.

"Look, Mummy," Lauren said pointing out toward the beach.

They were sitting around a large table on the outdoor deck overlooking the beach. A light morning rain had given way to a bright sun-kissed beach.

Lea looked up to where her daughter was pointing. A full, clear rainbow had formed over the ocean ending right where they were seated, a full multicolor arc that seemed to guide them over the ocean and into the other end.

"It's beautiful," Lea said with a sigh resting her head on her husband's shoulder while holding her son's hand.

She closed her eyes and took a deep breath, breathing in her life, breathing in her loved ones, and making space to feel and be present in the love around her.

* *

ABOUT DOLORES HIRSCHMANN

Dolores Hirschmann is a Writer, Coach, & Speaker.

New Beginnings... is her first novel. A writer from a young age, through this novel Dolores aims to share a story of finding new meaning, new ways to live one's life and start over. As a coach working with people "starting" their lives, their businesses, their new careers, Dolores supports them in finding their essence, their spark, and encourages them to build their lives from there. Originally from Argentina, Dolores lives in Massachusetts with her husband and four children.

You can reach Dolores at www.doloreshirschmann.com

Dolores Hirschmann